Was Henry Vidal's empire tottering? His house on Paradise Largo was hired – so were his six cars (including a Rolls) and his yacht. His six TV sets and five electronic typewriters were also hired – even his wife's jewellery. So far, he'd always paid on the nail – but the word was going round that Vidal's credit wouldn't hold out much longer . . . Clay Burden felt uneasy about having joined Vidal's outfit. It was Val's idea – the lovely, frightened Mrs Vidal, who'd meant everything to Clay six years ago. Now Clay had found her again, he didn't mean to let her go . . . even if it meant jeopardising his career . . . or resorting to desperate measures to free Val from the spell cast over her by her strange, dwarfish husband . . .

Also by James Hadley Chase

and published by Corgi Books

James Hadley Chase

Believe This—
You'll Believe Anything

CORGI BOOKS
A DIVISION OF TRANSWORLD PUBLISHERS LTD

BELIEVE THIS – YOU'LL BELIEVE ANYTHING

A CORGI BOOK 0 552 10275 X

Originally published in Great Britain by
Robert Hale and Company

PRINTING HISTORY
Robert Hale edition published 1975
Corgi edition published 1976

Copyright © James Hadley Chase 1975

This book is set in 10/10½ pt Baskerville.

Corgi Books are published by Transworld Publishers Ltd.,
Century House, 61–63 Uxbridge Road,
Ealing, London, W.5.
Made and printed in Great Britain by
Hunt Barnard Printing Ltd., Aylesbury, Bucks.

Believe This—
You'll Believe Anything

One

I saw him through the glass wall of my office as he came into the outer office. He was tall, lean, possibly in his early thirties, dark and immaculately dressed in a lightweight white suit that had been sculptured on him by the loving hands of an expert. Looking at his tanned profile, I decided he had to be a movie star. No movie producer would let a profile like this go without a struggle.

Sue Douglas, my woman Friday, was on her feet, giving him her big generous smile of welcome. Few men could resist Sue: she was one of those cuddly, warm attractive girls who make you think of Koala bears and who you want to stroke.

Her smile made no impact. He regarded her the way you would regard a fly that had dropped into your martini. Under his unfriendly stare, her smile wilted a little. He looked around the office until he saw me at my desk. We regarded each other through the glass wall, then side stepping Sue, he crossed to the door of my office and entered, closing the door gently behind him.

'Are you in charge here?' he demanded. That he was English, educated at Eton and Cambridge became immediately apparent. During my six months stay in England, I had learned something about the various class accents of the English and there was no mistaking this one.

'That's correct.' I got to my feet and gave him my version of a smile of welcome. 'Clay Burden. Something I can do for you?' I waved to the client's chair which he regarded suspiciously, then having satisfied himself it wouldn't spoil his beautiful white suit, he sank into it.

'You have just opened here?' he asked and glanced around critically.

'Yes . . . we have been open for exactly six days, Mr . . . ?'

He frowned at me, then lifted his elegant shoulders in a gesture that conveyed as plainly as if he had spoken, 'For God's sake, don't you even know who I am?'

'My name is Vernon Dyer. I suppose you wouldn't know that. I am extremely well known here.'

'You have the advantage of me.'

'I take it you are a newcomer to Paradise City?'

'Yes. I am from Boston, Mr Dyer.'

'I should have thought your agency would have chosen a local man.'

I let that one ride.

'Is there something I can do for you?'

If there was he appeared in no hurry to tell me.

'Is this all you have here: yourself and a girl?'

'That's all there is room for,' I said. 'The hotel would only spare so much space, but it is adequate.'

'I shouldn't have thought so. The American Express have a staff of fifteen.'

'Then they are not housed in the Spanish Bay hotel which is, as I am sure you know, the most exclusive hotel in the City.'

'I'm not interested in the hotel,' he said curtly. 'I am interested in getting a top class, travel agency service.'

'Then you have come to the right place, Mr Dyer. We don't handle the paper work here. We are here to give information, advice and so on while our head office in Miami issues tickets, traveller's cheques and in fact all the necessary paper work which comes to us by fast courier. For example, you may want to fly to New York. We can tell you the flights, book your seat, arrange for your ticket either to be delivered here or at Miami airport. This office gives personal advice. If that's what you are looking for, you will get it.'

He digested this as he crossed one leg over the other.

'I take it you will have heard of Mr Henry Vidal?'

I was now getting a little bored with his arrogance.

'Mr Henry Vidal? No, I'm afraid not. His fame so far hadn't reached Boston at the time I left,' I said. 'No one has mentioned the name to me since I arrived here so I have to admit Mr Vidal doesn't strike a note with me.'

He stared at me, not sure if I were conning him. I kept a bright look of interest on my face so he said, 'I would say Mr Vidal is the most important and influential man in Florida.'

'That puts him ahead of the Kennedys, Mr Nixon and the late Mr Truman,' I said gently. 'It is extraordinarily remiss of me not to have heard his name.'

Two tiny red spots showed on Dyer's thin cheeks and his eyes snapped.

'Are you being impertinent?'

'Not intentionally, Mr Dyer. Is there something I can do for you?'

He hesitated, then said, 'I am Mr Vidal's personal aide. Mr Vidal has decided to transfer his account from the American Express to your organisation. I can't imagine your organisation can be less efficient than the American Express. Let us hope not.'

'I'll be happy to do my best for Mr Vidal,' I said.

He studied me.

'You probably imagine that this account will be small and difficult, Mr Burden.'

Well, at least he had remembered my name.

'Small or large; difficult or easy makes no difference, Mr Dyer. We are here to give service.'

He put on his fly-in-his-martini expression.

'I hope so. Very well, consider yourself on trial. Open a checking account in the name of Vidal Enterprises. All transactions will be done through me on Mr Vidal's behalf.'

'Will you give me some idea of the amount of credit involved?'

'I have just closed our account with the American Express and settled their six monthly statement.' He paused, watching me, then said, 'The amount was one hundred and thirty thousand dollars.'

I stared at him, not believing I had heard aright. My startled expression seemed to give him immense satisfaction.

'Does that mean the account would be around two hundred thousand in a year?' I asked.

He flicked an invisible speck off his trouser knee.

9

'Yes . . . give and take. Could be more.'

I drew in a long, slow breath. This was an account I was not going to lose.

'You want the statements half yearly?'

'That is our method of payment.'

I wondered how head office would react to this, but if the American Express were content to carry Mr Henry Vidal for one hundred thousand for six months, the American Travel Services would probably do the same.

'I'll make immediate arrangements,' I said. 'There are naturally a few formalities . . . ' I let it die and looked at him.

'Of course.' He took from his wallet a folded sheet of paper. 'Here are the necessary details. Mr Vidal's address. The names and addresses of his attorney, his bankers and his brokers.' He put the paper on my desk. 'You will find everything in order. In the meantime, send me a schedule of flights for the next week to Tokyo, Johannesburg and Hong Kong. Two passengers to a flight, single. Everything V.I.P. They are to be met at the various airports by private car, to be at their disposal for six days. You will arrange luxe hotel accommodation also for six days, American plan. As soon as I get your estimate of the cost, I will give you further details. All correspondence should be addressed to me at Mr Vidal's residence. Have you got all that?'

I said I had.

He rose to his feet.

'Then good day to you.'

Without offering to shake hands, he left the office, swept past Sue without seeing her and made his way along the broad hotel corridor lined with boutiques, a drug store, a branch of Luce & Fremlin, the fashionable jewellers, Saks, Elizabeth Arden and the rest of them.

I watched him out of sight, then beckoned to Sue who came in.

'Who was that arrogant horror?' she asked.

'That was Vernon Dyer. We could be seeing a lot of him.' Briefly, I explained.

Her eyes popped wide open.

'Two hundred thousand?'

'That's what he said. Now to check.' I scribbled on a pad,

tore off the sheet and handed it to her. 'Get an estimate for this lot, Sue, with time schedules for next week.'

She nodded and returned to her desk.

I looked at my watch. The time was 12.35. Reaching for the telephone I called the American Express and asked for Joe Harkness, the district manager. We had already met and we liked each other. Although we were business rivals there was enough business for both agencies in Paradise City for us to remain relaxed and friendly with each other.

'Hi, Joe. This is Clay,' I said when he came on the line. 'How about eating a sandwich with me at the Howard Johnson?'

'If I think it is what it is, it's going to cost you more than a sandwich, buddy,' Harkness said cheerfully.

'Okay, you thief. Come on over and I'll buy you a steak in the grill room.'

'That's my boy. See you in half an hour,' and he hung up.

I studied the paper Dyer had given me.

Henry Vidal lived on Paradise Largo where only the very wealthy had residences. He had three banks: in Paradise City, in Miami and in New York. His attorney was Jason Shackman and his brokers were Trice, Seigler & Joseph.

I joined Sue at her desk.

'Just having a word with Rhoda,' I said, 'then I'm lunching with Harkness in the grill room.'

She nodded.

'I'll have this schedule and the estimate ready after lunch.'

I walked down the hotel corridor to The Trendie Miss boutique where Rhoda worked as one of the sales assistants. I found her alone, sitting on a stool, reading a woman's magazine – her favourite pastime.

Rhoda and I had been married now for just over two years. I had met her at the Statler Hilton, Boston at the time I was running the A.T.S. office there and she was assistant with The Trendie Miss boutique whose branches were in every major hotel in every major city. We had more or less drifted into marriage. She had a one room apartment in the high-rise where I lived. I got into the habit of driving her back from the hotel after work. There was a coffee shop in the complex and most nights we had dinner together there.

11

After a while, when we began sleeping together off and on, I picked up her check. She was young, attractive, gay and sexy. It was her idea we should get married. 'We'll economise,' she pointed out. 'I'll save rent.' She didn't tell me what I would save. I was getting tired of living on my own. I thought maybe if I married her, I would forget about Valerie; a stupid hope but I wanted very badly to forget the girl who had jilted me some four years ago. So I married Rhoda. I then made a depressing discovery. Although pretty, immaculately dressed when at work, her make-up a work of art, Rhoda was at heart a slut. Any kind of housework was her idea of hell. She wouldn't even make our bed. So I had to hire a woman to come in each day and we still ate our meals at the coffee shop.

When I got offered the Paradise City's A.T.S. office in the Spanish Bay hotel, Rhoda managed a transfer to The Trendie Miss boutique in the same lush hotel. Our combined earnings enabled us to live well, join the Country Club and even save money, but for me our marriage was no more than a sexual convenience combined with a tolerant association: not what I was hoping for.

'Rhoda,' I said, pausing in the shop's doorway, 'I can't lunch with you. I have a business date.'

She dragged her eyes from the magazine.

'Huh?'

'I have a business lunch,' I said patiently. I was used to repeating most things to Rhoda when she was reading.

'Oh? Well, okay. See you at six, huh?' She went back to her reading.

I took the elevator down to the grill room bar and ordered a Scotch on the rocks, something I seldom did at lunch time. As Sam, the barman, fixed the drink, I said, 'Ever heard of Mr Henry Vidal?'

'Vidal?' He set the drink before me. 'Can't say I have, Mr Burden.'

'I'm told he is the most influential man in Florida.'

He grinned.

'That depends who told you.'

Joe Harkness arrived five minutes later: a short thickset

12

man, around my own age, whose merry eyes and cheerful grin belied a shrewd business brain.

'That's for me,' he said pointing to my glass. 'Celebrating, Clay?'

'Maybe or recuperating.' I signalled to Sam. 'I've just had a visitor.'

'I know. I had him too. Well, Clay, ol'son, I'm sorry for you. When the s.o.b. told me he was closing the account with us, I jumped for joy.'

I stared at him.

'Don't try to con me, Joe.'

'It's a fact. I know it sounds cockeyed to be happy about losing an account worth two hundred thousand, but that's what I am. I've had a gutfull of Vidal and Dyer. I've had them in my hair for eighteen months . . . enough's enough.'

'Are you telling me the account is really worth two hundred thousand?'

'Sure and it is creeping up. That was last year's figure; could be more this year, but don't imagine you have a bonanza: let me disillusion you.' He drank half the whisky, then went on, 'Vidal insists on six month's credit. In other words he has the use of our money – around one hundred thousand – for six months. This he invests at seven per cent: that gives him three thousand five hundred per six months which we lose, not having the money, before he has to pay us. He also insists on a five per cent discount on all business over fifteen thousand per six months we handle for him and that gives him three thousand seven hundred and fifty which we also lose. So at the end of six months the one hundred thousand dollars of business we have handled for him only costs him ninety-two thousand seven hundred and fifty and we're out seven thousand two hundred and fifty which in a full year comes to around fifteen thousand.'

I grinned at him.

'So what? You made the terms. The account is still big. What are you beefing about?'

'Yeah . . . what am I beefing about? I'll tell you. We wanted the account and we expected to pay for it. We reckoned even with a five per cent discount and giving him six months' credit we could still make a fair profit, but how

13

wrong we were!' He laid his hand on my arm. 'We don't want that steak to spoil, do we?'

I paid for the drinks and we went into the grill room.

'Since this is on your expense account, Clay, don't let's cut corners,' Harkness said as he settled at the table. 'I'll take smoked salmon and french fries with the steak, and how about a nice bottle of something?'

I told the *Maître d'* to make it two smoked salmons, two steaks and a bottle of California red.

'Not Bordeaux?' Harkness said, looking pained.

'I haven't got the account yet. Were you telling me you don't make a profit out of Vidal?'

'I won't say that, but we'll be lucky to make two per cent which isn't good enough if you add the headaches and by God! there are plenty.'

'Such as?'

'I lost the best secretary I ever had – she quit after five months of Vernon. There is also the expense of keeping Vernon sweet. Then there was an assault case we had to settle out of court. Apart from these little things, Vernon is always belly aching. He's never satisfied.'

The waiter placed plates of smoked salmon before us.

'What assault case?'

Harkness grinned.

'One of my reps, goaded beyond endurance, punched Vernon's nose. Vernon sued. We settled for five thousand and lost a damn good rep.'

'What's this about keeping Vernon sweet?'

'He never comes to the office. Always meets me at one of the most expensive restaurants when he wants to discuss business and he always leaves me to pick up the tab. I guess I must have spent well over four thousand dollars in eighteen months of feeding that s.o.b.'

We ate for a few minutes while I thought over what he had told me.

'And Vidal? How do you react to him?'

'Never seen him. All I know about him is he has a hell of a place on Paradise Largo, owns a yacht, a Rolls convertible, a pretty wife and lots and lots of the green stuff. I've never

14

set eyes on him. He only circulates in the very best circles. Our Vernon does the slumming for him.'

'How does Vidal make his money?'

Harkness finished his smoked salmon and sat back with a sigh of content.

'He supplies demands.'

'Come again. What does that mean?'

'He has two hundred or so picked men working for him. They're on the move all the time which explains the size of his travel account. From what I'm told, half these men are hunting for people who have a surplus of any damn thing: sugar, coffee, nickel, oil, ships ... any damn thing. The other half are hunting for people who want these things. Vidal then gets the interested parties together, engineers the deal and picks up a fat commission. It's a nice way to earn a living, only you have to know who wants what and who has what to sell. Vidal seems to have built up an expert organisation that really delivers. The other day I read in the paper that Libya has bought a number of obsolete destroyers from England. I'll bet Vidal was behind that deal that has to be worth millions.'

I was impressed.

'Dyer asked me for a schedule ... '

Harkness held up his hand.

'Don't tell me. Let me guess. Tokyo, Jo'burg and Hong Kong. Right?'

I stared at him. 'Go on ... tell me more.'

'That's Vernon's first ploy to see what kind of job you'll do and how much you're going to charge him. He pulled that one on me. I got out the schedule which was never used. When he means business, he'll meet you for lunch. You'll get nothing out of Vernon for free.'

'Is the money safe?'

'That's the least of your worries. Vidal always pays up on the nail.'

'Did you take up references?'

'Oh, sure: all three banks and the brokers ... immaculate. I'll let you have photocopies if you want them.'

'Do that, will you, Joe?'

15

The steaks arrived.

'Let's forget about business,' Harkness said. 'Let's concentrate on these fine looking bits of bull.'

We ate for a while, then he said, 'When are you going to give me a game of golf, Clay?'

'If you're really looking for a beating, how about Sunday?' He grinned.

'Fine. Let's make it early. Nine o'clock?'

As Rhoda didn't get up until midday on Sundays this would give me time to get back to prepare a late brunch. Rhoda had no idea how to cook and refused to learn and as I refused to go to the coffee shop on Sundays I got landed with the brunch and supper.

After coffee, we parted.

As Harkness got in his car, he said, 'Any other little thing you want to know about Vidal give me a call.' He shook his head. 'Man, I'm sorry for you. I really mean it.'

He drove away leaving me feeling slightly uneasy.

* * *

Back in my office, I put a call through to Humphrey Massingham, the A.T.S. district general manager who was located in Miami. I told him about the Vidal account.

'That's an account I have had my eye on for some time, Clay,' he said, his voice excited. 'I never thought he would move from the American Express.'

'Harkness is happy to see him go,' I said. 'Could be we're getting ourselves a headache.'

'Two hundred thousand! I knew it was big, but not that big! We can take a lot of headaches for that amount of scratch.'

'You mean I can.'

He laughed.

'All part of the job,' he said airily, 'but you'll need extra help. I'll want you to concentrate on Vidal's account. I'll look around. We can afford additional staff now we have Vidal.'

'Don't be too sure you have him.' I went on to tell him

16

Vidal's likely terms and what Harkness had said. This damped his enthusiasm a little.

'Yeah . . . well, maybe we had better wait to see how you make out. You don't know he'll insist on those terms with us.'

'You can bet Dyer will try to screw us for even a bigger discount.'

'Five is our limit. Be firm with him.'

'I'll wait his first move. In the meantime, we should check the references, shouldn't we?'

'Oh, sure, but Vidal is big: one of the biggest. I'm sure there's no problem from that angle. I'll handle the references.'

'You might query the Credit Rating people. Bankers' references don't mean much.'

There was a pause, then he asked, 'Is something bothering you about this?'

'I'm not all that enthusiastic. I don't know why. Harkness said he was sorry for us and he meant it. I don't like Dyer.'

'That doesn't mean the money isn't sound. You leave it to me,' and he hung up.

As I replaced the receiver, Sue came in with the estimate and schedule Dyer wanted. We went through it together. As usual with her work I couldn't find faults.

'Fine, Sue.' I dictated a letter to Dyer, adding that formalities for opening the account were in hand and I would be writing him again. 'Mail it right away, will you? Let's show him we are on our toes.'

We spent the rest of the afternoon with routine work. We were kept busy until around 17.40. At the approach of cocktail time, inquiring tourists dropped away and gave us the chance to clear our desks. At 18.00 Sue said good night and hurried off home. I went along to the Trendie Miss to pick up Rhoda. She was completing a sale so I hung around in the corridor until she joined me.

'God! My feet!' she moaned as we walked across to the parking lot. 'It's fine for you, sitting all day, but I never get a chance to sit down.'

I didn't remind her she had been sitting down reading a magazine when I had cancelled our lunch together. I was

2

used to her moans. If it wasn't one thing, it was another.

'Want to go to a movie tonight?' I asked as we got into Plymouth.

'There's nothing worth seeing. I looked.' She settled herself and kicked off her shoes. 'This humidity drives me nuts. Put the air conditioner on for God's sake!'

I put it on. At this time of the season the heat and humidity was bad but not so bad as in Miami. As I drove out of the lot and headed home, I said, 'Ever heard of Henry Vidal?'

'Mrs Vidal was in yesterday. She bought belts and slacks. Our other lines are too young for her.'

'What is she like?'

Rhoda glanced at me.

'Why the interest?'

'Her husband opened an account with us worth two hundred thousand a year.'

'Wow!' Rhoda was always impressed with big money. 'Are you getting a rake-off, Clay?'

'No, he is. Did you see him?'

'She was on her own.'

'What's she like?'

Rhoda sniffed. I've never known her to praise any woman or consider any woman to be as smart as herself.

'All right, I guess, providing you like them slinky and dark. She knows how to dress. I'll say that for her.'

'All right to deal with?'

'I guess. She doesn't throw her weight around if that's what you mean; not like most of the hags who drive me nuts.'

'Pay cash?'

'She has a charge account.'

'Prompt payer?'

'How do I know? Who cares anyway? Do hurry it up, Clay. I can't wait to get under the shower.'

An hour later, Rhoda was lying on the balcony that overlooked the canal, a martini in one hand and a magazine in the other. I had taken a shower and now mixed myself a Scotch and soda. I joined her on the balcony. I knew I wouldn't get a word from her until it was time to go down to the coffee shop for dinner. I would have liked to have talked to her about Vidal Enterprises, to tell her about Vernon

Dyer, but I knew she wouldn't be interested. She was interested in little else except magazines and clothes.

Sitting opposite her, I thought how completely unlike Valerie she was.

Valerie had always been interested in anything I had done. She had a shrewd, intelligent mind and I had always discussed my business problems with her and she had always come up with useful suggestions.

Valerie!

Six years ago, I had become manager of the A.T.S. office in the Statler Hilton, Boston. Roy Cannon, the out-going manager (he had been transferred to New York) had met me at the airport. I had flown in from Cincinnati where I had been running the A.T.S. office at the Terrace Hilton. We had stopped in at the airport bar for a drink and to get to know each other.

'The one thing – and the only thing – that gripes me leaving Boston,' Cannon said as we propped up the bar, 'is losing the best secretary I've ever had. My loss, your gain. She's priceless and I'm not kidding. Never a moan if we work late, gorgeous to look at, terrific memory, fixes everything for you ... you can't imagine.'

Although I didn't believe Cannon's eulogy, I quickly discovered he hadn't been exaggerating. Valerie Dart was everything he had said she was: tall, with long, raven black hair, big blue eyes and a wide generous mouth: she was a beauty and her efficiency was unbelievable.

Within a few days I was in love with her, but although she was friendly, there was that little coolness that warned me not to rush my fences. We worked together from 09.30 until 18.00 which meant I saw more of her than I would have done had we been married. She had her own car and when we left the office, she would give me a smile and a wave and drive away. I had no part of her private life. She never discussed what she did in her spare time. Her coolness and her correct behaviour kept me at a distance.

Finally, with thumping heart, I asked her to have dinner with me. She had looked startled, and then had smiled. 'Thank you: that would be nice.'

I took her to a good sea-food restaurant and between

19

courses, we danced: still the coolness and I was on my best behaviour. It became a regular thing to take her out to dinner every Friday night, but when I suggested a movie on Wednesday night, she politely refused.

By then I had her in my blood like a virus. I knew there could be no other woman for me. She was the one, and even if I had to wait and wait, she would still be the one.

I stepped up the pace by giving her flowers and candy. I made the excuse it was my way of expressing appreciation for the way she helped me in the office.

Then one Friday night, some three months after I had met her, while we were dancing, I couldn't hold back any longer.

'Val,' I said. 'I'm in love with you. I think you must have guessed it by now. Could you think of marrying me? It's what I want more than anything else in the world. I just know we could be happy together. Tell me how you feel about me. Have I a chance?'

She rested her head against my shoulder so I couldn't see her face and we continued to dance for a few minutes, then she looked up and smiled at me. That smile made my heart leap.

'Yes, Clay, you have a chance, but I don't want to get married yet.'

I led her off the dance floor, out of the restaurant and on to the jetty, dimly lit by the moon.

'Are you telling me I mean something to you, Val?' I couldn't believe it.

'You do mean something to me.' She kissed my cheek. 'But don't rush me. Let's wait a while. If I marry you, I would want to run your home. I don't want to give up the office for a while. Please be patient with me.'

I was too happy to sleep that night.

The following morning, I had a call from head office. Vice-President John Ryner wanted to see me. Wondering what it was all about, I left Val to take charge of the morning stint – it was Saturday and we closed at 13.00 – and flew down to New York.

Ryner received me cordially and came straight to the point.

'Clay, it's time you took a look at the European scene.

We've arranged for you to work at our branch in London for six months and in our Paris branch for another six months. Take the chance to polish up your French while you're in Paris. More and more people are visiting London and Paris, and for you to be efficiently helpful you must know the up-to-date scene. I'm putting Bill Olson in your place at the Statler Hilton, but the job will be waiting for you on your return with a fifteen hundred raise. When can you get off?'

I did some quick thinking. The last thing I wanted was to be parted from Val, but she had told me she wanted time before we married and I knew she wouldn't be rushed. With a fifteen hundred increase, we could live pretty comfortably.

I said I would go when he wanted me to go.

'Tuesday?'

'Okay.' It was rushing it, but the sooner I left, the sooner I would be back.

'Fine.' I could see he was pleased. 'Olson will be up on Monday. Miss Dart can show him the ropes.' He looked at me. 'She's a damn good secretary, isn't she?'

'The best.' I wondered how he would react if I broke the news that the agency might be losing her.

Before leaving New York, I called Boston and just managed to catch Val as she was shutting the office.

'I'll be back at four, Val,' I said. 'I must talk to you. Can you meet the plane?'

'Yes, of course.'

I had an hour before my flight. I went to a nearby jeweller's shop and bought an engagement ring: two emeralds and a diamond. I had it gift wrapped, then took a taxi to the airport.

Val was waiting for me. As we walked together to the parking lot where she had left her VW, she asked, 'What was it all about, Clay?'

'Big deal,' I said, smiling at her. 'Let's drive to Franklin park. Now tell me about your morning. Anything happen?'

She could see I didn't want to talk until we could be somewhere quiet so while she drove she told me of the morning's activities. Business had been brisk and she had finally persuaded an elderly couple to go on a world tour. They had

21

been nibbling at the bait for some time and I had almost given them up.

We left the car and walked through the rose gardens in the park until we found a deserted bench. We sat in the sun and I told her what Ryner wanted me to do.

'I hate leaving you, Val,' I said, 'but this will give you the chance to make up your mind. I'll be away a year. When I get back, I hope you'll be all set to marry me. I wouldn't do this if it wasn't for the raise. An extra fifteen hundred will come in handy to set up home, won't it?'

She looked searchingly at me.

'I'll miss you, Clay.'

I gave her the ring. When she had unwrapped it and opened the little box, she caught her breath, then looked at me, her eyes scared.

'I can't accept this, Clay. No . . . it's too binding. Please . . .' She thrust the box at me, but I wouldn't take it. 'It's sweet of you, but anything can happen in a year. I think I love you, but I do want to be sure. I don't want to feel tied.'

I was disappointed by her reaction, but I didn't show it.

'You won't be tied. Wear it on your right hand to please me. When you have made up your mind, put it on your left hand. What's wrong with that as an idea?'

'It's a beautiful ring.' She regarded it for a long moment, then took it from the box and slipped it on the third finger of her right hand. 'There . . . does that please you?' She leaned forward and we kissed. 'Now, I am going to cook dinner for you,' she went on. 'I want you to know I'm just as efficient in the home as I am at the office.'

We drove back to the City, and she bought the ingredients for dinner, then she drove me to her complex.

It was a beautifully kept apartment and the dinner was superb.

We talked long into the night and when I finally left, we arranged to spend the following day – Sunday – at the Sailsbury Beach reservation. It was the happiest and most wonderful week end I had ever had.

On Tuesday, leaving Bill Olson at my desk, Val went with me to the airport to see me off.

'Wait for me, Val,' I said. 'It's only for a year. Then we can set up home.'

But it wasn't to be. I wrote every day. She had warned me she was no good as a letter writer and I didn't get many letters from her. What I did get were affectionate and she seemed happy.

After six months in London, I moved to Paris. I found a furnished one-room apartment near the office and wrote, giving Val my new address. I hadn't heard from her for the past three weeks and I was getting worried. A week later, just as I was about to telephone her, a registered packet arrived. In it I found the engagement ring and a brief note:

Dear Clay,
I am leaving Boston for good. I hate hurting you, but I must tell you there is someone else. There will be someone else for you too. I'm sorry. It happened so suddenly. Forgive me and forget me.

Val.

I was in a pretty bad way for some months. I did my work automatically, resisted the temptation to get drunk every night and led a lonely, miserable life. Finally, I returned to Boston. I asked Olson, as soon as we met, if he could explain why Val had thrown up her job.

'Not an idea, Clay,' he said. 'I wish I had. She said she was leaving for personal reasons: that's all. You know how remote she can be. I just had to accept it.'

Four years drifted by. The ache was continuous. Then I met Rhoda. I wanted desperately to lead a normal life again and to forget Val, but my marriage to Rhoda proved no solution. It was now six years since I received the letter that took the fun and happiness out of my life and the ache for Val was still with me.

'Clay!'

I started. My mind had been so occupied with the past I had forgotten Rhoda.

'I'm hungry.' She swung her pretty legs off the lounging chair. 'What's biting you? You look like something the cat's sicked up.'

'Let's eat,' I said. 'Nothing's biting me.'

I had never told her about Val. She had never asked me if there had been any other woman before I met her. She just wasn't interested enough to bother with the past. The present was as much as she could cope with.

We went down to the coffee shop for the inevitable hot dogs and then returned to the apartment for the inevitable goggle box yawn until bed time.

Two

THE FOLLOWING morning, as I was going through the mail, Humphrey Massingham telephoned.

'I've checked out Vidal,' he said. His voice lacked its usual breezy tone. 'The bankers, of course, give a glowing report and so do the brokers. That was a smart idea of yours to query the Credit Rating people. Believe it or not, Vidal doesn't seem to own a thing! I don't know if it means anything, but it is odd. The house, furnished is hired, his six cars, including the Rolls and the yacht are hired. He has six TV sets in the house as well as five electronic I.B.M. typewriters – all hired. Even his wife's jewellery is hired from Luce & Fremlin and he changes the stuff every month. The Credit Rating people tell me he has six month's credit with all these creditors and he pays on the nail when the accounts come due. What do you make of it?'

'A pretty convenient arrangement if you want to skip suddenly,' I said.

'That's right. I got the same thought. I queried Mr Ryner. He's talked to one of the A.E. directors who admits they are glad to get rid of Vidal's account because of its nuisance value and the big discount, but says there's nothing wrong with Vidal money-wise. Ryner also talked to other leading travel agencies. Apparently Dyer has approached a number of them before us but they turned him down. They're not big enough to carry Vidal for six months. Ryner says if you can talk Dyer out of the five per cent discount, we go ahead, but we don't if Dyer won't play.'

'Do we give him six months' credit?'

'I guess so. All Vidal's other creditors are giving him that. It seems to me we have Dyer where we want him. He either accepts our terms or he is without an agency. We seem to be his last chance for a deal.'

'Fine. Okay, leave him to me.'

A little after 10.30, Vernon Dyer came on the line.

'I've got your schedule,' he said, a rasp in his voice. 'What's the idea? What do you think you're playing at? Your prices are ten per cent ahead of the American Express quotation.'

'They quoted you eighteen months ago, Mr Dyer,' I said smoothly. 'Prices have gone up since then and they are likely to keep going up. The price I've quoted you is present day rock bottom.'

There was a pause, then he said, less sharply, 'Those formalities completed yet?'

'Yes. The account is now open.'

'Then we had better get together and talk terms. Be at the Coq d'Or restaurant at 13.00. Right?'

The Coq d'Or restaurant was the most expensive and exclusive restaurant in Paradise City. It cost you $1.50 just to check your hat.

'Thank you for the invitation, Mr Dyer, but you must excuse me,' I said blandly. 'I never go out to lunch. I'll be here any time convenient to you.'

'You never go out to lunch?' His voice shot up. 'What do you mean?'

'I take a desk lunch, Mr Dyer. I'm too busy to eat out.'

'Harkness always lunched with me!'

'That was his privilege. When do you think you could drop in, Mr Dyer?'

There was a long pause, then he said, 'I think you should have the courtesy to lunch with me.'

'It's not a matter of courtesy, it's a matter of having the time, Mr Dyer. You want top class service: by having a desk lunch, I am able to give it to you.'

'Oh, very well!' I could tell by the tone of his voice he was angry and frustrated. 'Then this afternoon at 15.00,' and he hung up.

I looked over at Sue and winked at her.

'No more expensive lunches for Vernon,' I said. 'We're getting away to a good start.'

Dyer didn't show up until 16.00. I was busy with a client and he paced up and down outside my office. From time to time, he paused to glare at me and look at his watch. I paid no attention. When my client left, I waved to Dyer to come in.

'Sorry to have kept you, but your appointment was for 15.00.'

He grunted and sat down.

'So the account's open,' he said. 'I take it you have talked to Harkness?'

'I've talked to him.'

'We'll be satisfied with the same terms as we got from him.' He stared at me. 'You know the terms?'

'I know them but unfortunately we can't accept them.'

He stiffened.

'What the hell do you mean? What's good enough for the American Express is surely good enough for you.'

'The arrangement you made with them was eighteen months ago, Mr Dyer. We are trying to keep prices down. We can still give you six months' credit, but I regret no discount.'

He leaned forward, his face flushed, his eyes glittering.

'So you don't want our business?'

'I didn't say that, Mr Dyer.'

'That's just what you are saying! You either give us the same terms as the American Express gave us or you don't get our business!'

'Then regretfully we don't get it.' I put on a sad expression. 'If you are able to find another agency who will give you the terms you want, Mr Dyer, then obviously it is your privilege to go to them.'

He sat back, glaring.

'Are you serious? Are you telling me you won't take business worth two hundred thousand for the sake of an absurd five per cent discount?'

'Which would amount to ten thousand in your favour. I'm sorry, Mr Dyer, that's the way it is.'

He licked his lips, then asked in a more conciliatory tone, 'What will you give – four per cent?'

I knew then he was bluffing.

'I'm sorry, but there can be no discount.' I smiled at him. 'Have you tried the Global or the Florida agencies?'

'They're useless!' By his flush I knew he had tried them.

'There are plenty of others. I'll ask Miss Douglas to give you a list of them if that would be helpful.'

He sat for some moments, staring down at his hands, then he said, 'You will give us six months' credit?'

'That's agreed.'

'It's most odd you can't give some kind of discount on a turnover like this.'

'I'm sorry.'

He shrugged and forced a smile.

'Okay, I suppose you had better have the account.'

'That's up to you, Mr Dyer.'

He took out a gold cigarette case, selected a cigarette and lit it.

'How about my commission?'

I lifted my eyebrows.

'Excuse me . . . your commission?'

His eyes snapped angrily.

'You don't expect me to give you an account of this size without you giving me something in return? It's normal business practice.'

'What had you in mind, Mr Dyer?'

His face lit up.

'Five thousand would be acceptable . . . in cash, of course.'

For sheer nerve and effrontery, I thought, this arrogant creep wanted beating.

'I'll take it up with head office,' I said.

His eyes shifted.

'This would be strictly confidential, of course.'

'I doubt if my people would consider it as such. It's a practice my people don't approve of.' I gave him my sympathetic smile. 'As far as I'm concerned if someone gets a pay off for bringing an account to us, I say good luck to him.'

He gave me a leering little smile.

'I'm sure you can handle this for me, Burden. Of course

Mr Vidal need not know. You understand? After all I am doing you a favour.'

'My Vice-President is a little sticky, Mr Dyer. If he hears Mr Vidal's personal aide is asking us for five thousand dollars for bringing Mr Vidal's account to us, it is rather likely he would write to Mr Vidal to ask if he approved.'

Dyer lost colour.

'You mean I don't get anything?'

'Service, Mr Dyer. You'll get that.'

He really hated me then. I could see it in the expression in his eyes. With an unsteady hand he took an envelope from his pocket and threw it on my desk.

'Here are your instructions! Get working on them! And I warn you, Burden, no slip-ups! I don't tolerate shoddy work!'

Getting to his feet, he stalked out of my office, past Sue and away down the corridor.

I opened the envelope and studied his instructions. It was a nice order: six first class fares New York–Tokyo: hotel accommodation for fourteen days, chauffeur driven car, everything V.I.P.

I put the instructions back in the envelope, told Sue to get it to Miami by special messenger, then returning to my office, I called Massingham and gave him a blow-by-blow account of my interview with Dyer.

When he was through laughing, he said: 'Fine, Clay. I'll tell Mr Ryner. You couldn't have done better. We'll cope with the Tokyo schedule as soon as we get it. Don't tell Harkness about this. Let's keep it under our hats.'

I did tell Sue. I wanted to tell Rhoda as we drove home. I felt like crowing a little about this triumph, but I knew Rhoda wouldn't be interested. She was again moaning about her feet.

But Val would have been interested. She would have insisted we celebrated this little triumph.

The ache began again.

*　　*　　*

The Tokyo schedule, the air tickets and the hotel vouchers arrived in the morning's mail. Around 10.00, I called Dyer at the Vidal residence. After some delay, he came on the line.

'I have the Tokyo schedule wrapped up,' I said. 'Shall I mail it to you or will you arrange to have it picked up?'

'Bring it here yourself,' he snapped. 'I have more business to discuss with you. I'm not wasting my time in the future, hanging around your office,' and he slammed down the receiver.

I should have expected that. It was his petty way of getting even. Now it would be his turn to keep me waiting.

I left my office to consult Sue.

'Unless we have a rush,' she said, 'I'm sure I can manage.'

'But we could have a rush. I don't want complaints. We have assured the hotel, in return for this office space, we would give them top class service. I'll talk to Massingham.'

Massingham was immediately alive to the situation.

'Remember Bill Olson from Boston?' he said. 'He's just arrived here to get the background of Florida. I'll send him to you. He may as well work with you as with me. He'll be over in an hour.'

I was startled. I hadn't seen Olson since Val had left Boston so mysteriously. Remembering him made me think of her again.

I told Sue.

'Fix it we get another desk in here,' I said. 'I guess if you move your desk further to the left, we can just squeeze in a second.'

She nodded.

'I'll fix it right away,' and reached for the telephone.

Taking the schedule and the tickets, I went down the corridor towards the parking lot. I looked in at The Trendie Miss. Rhoda was sitting on her stool, absorbed in a magazine.

'Watch it, honey,' I said, 'or you'll wear your feet out.'

She looked up blankly.

'Huh?'

'Nothing. I may not be back in time for lunch. Don't wait for me. I'm calling on Mr Henry Vidal.'

'Big deal, huh?' and she returned to her magazine.

Paradise Largo is an isthmus linking E.1 to A.1.A highways. The causeway leading to the Largo is guarded by a lodge and an electronically controlled barrier. No one –

repeat no one – is allowed on the Largo without first identifying himself and stating his business.

Hidden behind high flowering hedges, some three feet thick and guarded by big oak, nail studded gates, are some thirty to forty magnificent houses owned by the wealthiest of Florida's wealthy.

I stopped the Plymouth before the lodge and submitted to a searching stare by the blue uniformed guard.

'Calling on Mr Dyer at Mr Vidal's residence,' I said. 'The name's Clay Burden. Mr Dyer is expecting me.'

'Driving licence,' he said.

I gave it to him, and after examining it, he handed it back, then turning away, he reached for a telephone. There was a delay, then he pressed a button that lifted the barrier and he waved me through.

'Fourth gates on your left.'

I drove down the wide, sand strewn road, turned left and arrived at a massive twelve foot high set of gates which were opened by another blue uniformed guard.

'Straight ahead, Mr Burden,' he said. 'Park in lot 4.'

I drove up the winding drive shaded by palm trees and lined on either side with Sweet Bay and Oleander shrubs. A half acre of immaculate lawn and flower beds, blazing with colour, appeared on my right, then I saw the house, a two-storey, Spanish style building covered with red and pink Bougainvillaea. There was a loggia running the length of the house, decorated with pink coral stone. A lush place: big, imposing and opulent.

I parked in lot 4 as directed, On one side of me was a Rolls Corniche and on the other a Lamborghini Espada. Their glittering coach work made my Plymouth look shabby.

A dark skinned flunkey in white linen trousers and a blood red jacket moved out of the shade and showed me his teeth.

'Mr Burden?'

I nodded.

'This way, please.'

He led me along a path lined on either side with red azalea shrubs that made a splendid ribbon of colour to a long, low building of white wood. He pushed open a door, stood aside as he said, 'Third door, please. I will tell Mr Dyer.'

I entered a large room with a big oval table in the centre, covered with magazines. There were eight men, fat, thin, middle aged and elderly, all wearing City suits, sitting in lounging chairs, brief cases on their knees. They looked sharply at me as if suspecting I was a dangerous competitor, then when I sat down, they looked away.

We all sat in silence. After five minutes, a woman's voice said through a concealed speaker, 'Mr Hedger please. Room five.'

A fat, elderly man sprang to his feet and hurried out.

More minutes dragged by, another name was called, another man hurried out.

This went on until only a balding man and I were left.

'Like being at the dentist,' I said, lighting my fourth cigarette.

'That's right. I guess I prefer the dentist any day.' He took out a handkerchief and mopped his sweating face.

I glanced at my watch. I had been sitting there now for an hour and ten minutes. Next time, if there was a next time, I told myself, I would bring some work to do.

The balding man was called. He nodded to me on his way out.

An hour and thirty-five minutes later, my name was called.

'Mr Burden please. Room fifteen.'

I found Vernon Dyer lounging behind a vast desk cluttered with three telephones, a tape recorder, an intercom with about thirty switches, a bowl of flowers, a bowl of salted peanuts, three onyx ash trays, a silver cigarette box and a small cigar cabinet. It was a wonder to me he had room to write a letter. Maybe he didn't. Maybe he nibbled peanuts and dictated.

'There you are,' he said laughing. 'Sit down.'

I put the wallet containing the schedule, air tickets and hotel vouchers on the blotter before him, then sat down.

He took his time examining the schedule, obviously trying to find fault. He looked up suddenly, scowling.

'Why put them in at the Pacific hotel?' he demanded.

'It has a fine garden, a Japanese atmosphere and it's much quieter than the Imperial.'

'They won't have time to use the garden and who the hell

cares about atmosphere? Put them up at the Imperial!'

'No problem, Mr Dyer.'

He glared at me.

'I want the vouchers by 16.00 and not later.'

'You'll have them. Maybe next time you will tell me the hotel you prefer.'

'It's your job to know the best hotels!'

'In my opinion the Pacific is the best.'

He flushed.

'Change it to the Imperial.' He tossed the hotel vouchers over to me, then looked at the wall clock. The time was 13.10. 'Is it as late as that?' He paused to give me a sneering little smile. 'I'll have to ask you to come back. I have a lunch date. Be at 15.00. Right?'

I got to my feet.

'I have an appointment at 15.00, Mr Dyer. I'm sorry.'

He cocked his head on one side and squinted at me.

'With an account our size, I expect service. I want you here at 15.00.'

'Still sorry. If it's that urgent why don't you come to my office after your lunch?'

We stared at each other. His eyes were the first to shift. His face was tight with anger as he said, 'All right. All right. I'm late as it is so I may as well be later. I'll give you instructions now.' He took from his desk drawer a heavy envelope and handed it to me. 'Go through this. Call me tomorrow if there are any queries . . . there probably will be. Don't make out any hotel vouchers without consulting me.'

'Okay,' I said and moved to the door.

'Wait. I was forgetting. I want you to be completely available for five days from next Tuesday.'

'Completely available?' I repeated, staring at him.

'That's what I said. Mr Vidal is going to San Salvador. Mrs Vidal is going with him. While Mr Vidal is occupied with business, you are to take Mrs Vidal around and show her the sights. Everything V.I.P. of course. Air conditioned cars: a suite at the hotel. Mr Vidal wants to stay at the Intercontinental. First class air for them: economy for you. The full instructions are in the envelope.'

This was something I didn't want to do. I knew I would

be useless as a guide, not having been to El Salvador, and besides, it wasn't my job.

'We have a good agency in San Salvador who will take excellent care of Mrs Vidal.'

'That is just what Mr Vidal doesn't want!' Dyer snapped. 'He said emphatically that Mrs Vidal was not to go around with some Latin-American dago. He wants you to do it. Any objections?'

'Valuable as Mr Vidal's account is, it isn't the only one I look after,' I said. 'I will see what can be arranged. We have a first class guide at Miami who would look after Mrs Vidal.'

'I told Mr Vidal you would be pleased to do the job so you had better do it!'

'If I am away for five days, there will be no one to look after your instructions.' I was threshing around to find an excuse.

'You have next week's instructions in your hand,' Dyer said impatiently. 'There won't be any other business until you get back.'

I gave up.

'I'll see what can be arranged,' I said and left him.

I stopped at a Howard Johnson restaurant for a prawn salad and a coke. While I ate, I went through the instructions he had given me. It was an impressive travel order: first class fare, plus hotel accommodation for a week for ten people on a sight-seeing trip to London. A similar trip for five people sight-seeing in Paris and a flight for two to Moscow. All V.I.P. Finally I came to Vidal's trip. He and his wife were to leave Monday and to be met at el Aeropuerto de Ilopango and conveyed in an air conditioned car to the Intercontinental hotel. I was to join them the following day, Tuesday, and take Mrs Vidal sight-seeing. I was to be at her disposal while they stayed in San Salvador. We were to return to Paradise City on Sunday.

I drove back to the office to find Bill Olson installed. Both he and Sue were tied up with clients.

Olson looked up and grinned at me. He had aged a little since we last met: a tall, rangy man with an easy manner, a ready smile and good features.

Not wanting to disturb him, I waved and went into my

office. I called Massingham. I told him about the Imperial hotel vouchers and asked him to have them sent to Dyer before 16.00, then went on to tell him about the El Salvador trip.

'If Dyer isn't going to bother us while you're away,' Massingham said, 'then I think you should go. It'll be a change of scene for you.'

'But I've never been there and will be useless as a guide.'

'Telex the San Salvador agency. Tell them to get out a sight-seeing schedule and for them to provide a chauffeur-guide. The Vidals can't object to him if you are with him, can they?'

'I shouldn't think so. Okay, I'll do that. When your messenger has delivered the vouchers, tell him to come on here. I've got more business for you and Dyer wants the schedules in a rush.'

Massingham swore under his breath.

'Now I can understand why A.E. consider him a nuisance.'

'It's a good order. You'll like it when you see it.'

'Okay. I'll get the schedules to you by tomorrow morning,' and he hung up.

I telexed the San Salvador agency. They replied that they would have everything laid on for the Vidals when they arrived and a chauffeur-guide to work with me.

It wasn't until 17.40 that I was able to leave my office and welcome Olson. As we shook hands, he grinned at me.

'Nice seeing you again, Clay,' he said. 'How long is it? Six years?'

'About that. How are you fixed, Bill? Where are you sleeping tonight?'

Olson looked over at Sue who was clearing her desk.

'That wonderful girl has already hired me a furnished apartment on Biscayne avenue.'

'That's right by my place. Look, Bill, let me clear my desk and we'll go back to my apartment for a drink and dinner. I want you to meet Rhoda, my wife.'

'Fine. There are just a couple of things I have to tie up, then I'll be ready.'

Rhoda always came alive when we had guests. She and Olson got on well together. I could see he was impressed by her prettiness and her smart clothes. I thought a little sourly, as I mixed a batch of martinis, he would have a shock if he saw her over the week-end when she slopped around the apartment without make-up, her hair looking like a bird's nest and in grubby jeans and grubbier sweater.

It was while I was pouring the drinks, Olson said casually, 'Did you ever see Val again after she walked out on us?'

I spilt a little of the drink and without looking up, I said, 'No, nor heard from her.'

Rhoda reached for some peanuts.

'Who is Val?' she asked curiously.

Olson grinned.

'Do you mean your hubby never told you about Val Dart?'

'He never tells me anything.' Rhoda pouted and took the glass I handed to her. 'What's so special about her?'

'You imagine I never tell you anything,' I said, handing Olson his glass, 'the fact is you never listen to anything I say.'

'Don't tell me you told me about her because I know you didn't!' There was a snap in her voice now.

'She wouldn't interest you anyway. She happened to be my secretary when I was at the Statler-Hilton before you arrived,' I said, trying to sound casual. 'Here's to you, Bill.'

We drank, then Olson said, 'And what a secretary! The most efficient, smart, gorgeous girl it's been my luck to work with!'

I could see Rhoda hated this. Anyone praising any woman made her bristle.

Looking directly at me, she said, 'I bet you loved her. Efficiency is your middle name.'

'Is it – ?' I walked over to the window and looked down at the canal. I loved her all right. I still loved her.

'I honestly don't know why Clay married me,' Rhoda said to Olson. 'He's always telling me how inefficient I am. He nags me from morn to night. Pity he didn't marry this Val who seems to be so gorgeous and efficient.'

The acid note in her voice made Olson look uncomfortable.

'I can't imagine you being inefficient, Mrs Burden,' he said awkwardly.

I wasn't going to support him. There was a pause, then

Rhoda said, 'Who cares anyway about efficiency? I think it's a great big bore. Who wants to mess around this apartment when we can get some old cow to do it? When you're through gawping out of the window, Clay, how about a refill?'

Again an awkward pause while I freshened the drinks, then Olson said, 'Sue was telling me about the Vidal account. You've certainly helped yourself to some trouble, haven't you, Clay?'

I shrugged.

'Massingham does all the work. I just listen to the complaints. I can take a lot of that.' I turned to Rhoda. 'That reminds me, honey, you're going to be a grass widow for six days next week.'

'What do you mean?'

I told her about the El Salvador trip.

I could see she was nonplussed. This would be the first time we had separated since we married.

'How about me?' Her voice shot up. 'How am I going to get to work and home again?'

'The bus stops right outside both ways.'

'Bus! Who wants to use the smelly bus?'

'I'll be happy to drive you, Mrs Burden,' Olson said. 'No problem. I'd be glad to.'

She flashed him a smile.

'Clay never considers me. Thanks, Bill. I may call you Bill? You call me Rhoda.'

'Fine.'

I wasn't surprised when she turned on me.

'So you're going away with that Vidal hag! She's just the type to try to drag you into her bed!'

I never have lost my temper with Rhoda no matter how irritating she was, but this time, I had to make an effort to control it.

'Come on, honey, let's skip this nonsense. I have a job to do, so there's no point in moaning.'

'I bet you'll enjoy it thinking of me slaving in that damn boutique.'

'Come the day when you do do some slaving.' I turned to Olson who was looking embarrassed. 'Hungry?'

'I guess. Whenever you say.'

'Are you ready, Rhoda?'

'No, I'm not!'

She got to her feet and walked into the bedroom, slamming the door.

Olson and I looked at each other.

'Women!' I forced a smile.

'Yeah.' A pause, then he said, 'Nice place you have here.' He moved out on to the balcony. 'Marvellous view.'

'That's a fact.'

With an obvious attempt to change the subject, Olson said, 'This guy Vidal . . . quite a man of mystery.'

'Would you call him that? He's certainly loaded.'

'He hadn't much five years ago. He used to be a client of mine at the Statler Hilton. In those days, he could only afford economy class. He wanted a checking account with us, but his credit rating wasn't sound.'

I stared at him.

'How come Massingham didn't know that?'

'I guess I didn't report it to New York. I checked with Credit Rating and they said better not, so I turned Vidal down. It never got on our records.'

'But Massingham has checked the Credit Rating people.' Olson laughed.

'This was five years ago, Clay. Lots of things can happen in five years. They probably didn't think it was necessary to tell Massingham we once turned him down.'

'Yeah. So you've met him. That's my doubtful privilege next Tuesday. What's he like?'

'An odd-ball. For one thing, he's almost a dwarf: under five foot and has all the usual aggressiveness of little men. He wears a beard and is balding, but he's a dynamo all right. You know the type: a real pusher, talks fast, waves his hands around, has hypnotic eyes. When I knew him he made a big commotion out of the simplest things. Booking a ticket to New York was a major thing with him. You would think he was taking a trip to the moon, but I guess he must have changed a lot since then. Rumour has it he's worth millions. When you amass that kind of bread you don't have to impress, you let your slaves do it for you.'

'How right you are,' and I told him about Dyer.

Rhoda came out of the bedroom. She still looked sulky.

'Are we going to eat, or aren't we?' she demanded. 'I'm hungry.'

'We're waiting for you, honey,' I said.

'Well, for heaven's sake, let's go somewhere decent for a change. I'm sick of the coffee shop.'

She flounced out of the apartment and after exchanging rueful grins, Olson and I followed her.

* * *

Rhoda was never happier than when, given the rare opportunity, she could score off me. Admittedly, I had been forced by her careless, sluttish ways to protest often enough and she hated any form of criticism. So scoring off me was always to her a major triumph.

It soon became apparent that she had been shrewd enough to guess that Val had made an impression on me and she grabbed at the chance to be irritating.

After we had driven Olson back to his apartment and we had returned home, I began clearing the table of the cocktail things. Moving past me, Rhoda managed to sweep the bowl of peanuts off the table with her shirt, scattering the nuts all over the carpet.

She had been in a difficult mood during dinner and my nerves were jumpy.

'Look what you've done! Careful how you walk,' I said sharply. 'You'll mess the whole carpet!'

'Go on, nag!' I could see she was furious with herself for being so clumsy. 'I bet your efficient, gorgeous Val didn't do things like that.'

If I had kept my cool and had ignored the remark, I wouldn't have given her the hint that the subject of Val, to me, was a touchy one.

'Oh, wrap up!' I said angrily. 'Why don't you look where you're going?'

She regarded me, gave a sudden little grin and went into the bedroom.

The next four days were trying. Apart from clearing my desk in preparation for my trip, coping with Dyer who was continually on the telephone raising stupid and unnecessary queries about the schedules he had given me and handling the day to day routine work, Rhoda became increasingly tiresome.

When she upset a box of face powder in the bathroom, leaving me to clear up the mess, she shook her head in mock sadness as she said, 'I really must try to be like efficient, gorgeous Val.' When she overslept and made me late for the office, she said, 'I'm sure gorgeous, efficient Val never kept you waiting.'

Every time she mentioned Val's name it was more than a pin prick to me. With an effort I kept my temper and ignored her jibes, hoping she would get tired of baiting me.

I now found myself looking forward to getting away from her for five days. She would probably have forgotten Val by the time I returned.

We took Olson out to dinner on Monday night and Rhoda was on her best behaviour. We had a pleasant evening, but returning to our apartment after dropping Olson off at his, Rhoda flopped into a lounging chair, lit a cigarette and surprised me by saying, 'Let's have a drink, Clay. A goodbye toast, huh?'

'Why not. Scotch?'

'Hmmmm.'

I fixed the drinks and sat opposite her.

'Tell me, Clay, was Val your mistress?'

I slopped my drink so violently some of the ice shot out of the glass on to the carpet.

Rhoda giggled.

'Who's clumsy now?'

I picked up the ice cubes and took them into the kitchen.

I stood for a moment or two to compose myself, then I returned to the living room, aware that Rhoda was watching me.

'Was she your mistress?' she repeated.

'No. Now listen, Rhoda, I've had enough of this. Understand? From now on you will cut out this continuous reference to Val. I don't know what the idea is, but if you think it is funny, I don't.'

She sipped her drink and eyed me over the rim of the glass.

'She did mean something to you, didn't she?' She giggled. 'I believe you're still in love with her.'

'Stop this nonsense! You're just showing what a small, stupid mind you have!'

She flushed.

'You don't deny it, do you?'

'There's nothing to deny. Finish your drink and let's go to bed.'

'Well, five days with slinky Mrs Vidal might cure you,' she said spitefully. 'She's just the kind who could get a faded romance out of your head. It would be a joke if you went all moody about her.'

Leaving my drink, I went into the bedroom. I was so angry that if I hadn't left her, I would have slapped her. She must have sensed she had gone too far for she remained in the living room until she heard the shower going, then she hurriedly undressed and was in bed by the time I came out of the bathroom.

'I was only kidding, Clay. Can't you take a joke?' she said, uneasily.

'You haven't cleaned your teeth,' I snapped. 'For God's sake hurry up! I want some sleep if you don't!'

'To hell with my teeth and to hell with you!' she exclaimed furiously and turning her back on me, she snapped off the light.

Three

I was met at el Aeropuerto de Ilopango by a stockily built, swarthy Indian who introduced himself as Roberto Rivera. He was in his middle forties with a Charlie Chan moustache, and he had the crafty eyes and the sly smile of the Latin-American at his worst. I took a dislike to him at first sight.

'Welcome, *Señor* Burden,' he said, shaking hands and raising his straw sombrero. 'Everything is very fine. I meet *Señor* Vidal and the *señora* as arranged. No problems. I am at your disposal. You wish to go to the hotel?'

'Yes, please. Is it far?'

'No distance: perhaps a little way. Here is the beautiful car, full air conditioned, every comfort, much expense.' He led me over to a dusty black Mercedes 200 parked in the sun and opened the offside door, again lifting his sombrero.

I was glad to get into the cool of the car. The sun must have been 96 in the shade.

He slid under the driving wheel.

'Excuse my English, *Señor* Burden. Speak very fine American, but English more difficult.'

I said I understood.

He drove away from the airport and along a dusty road crowded with Indian peasants. Nearly all of them carried big metal pots on their heads or their shoulders.

'What are they carrying?' I asked.

'Water, *Señor* Burden. Water is difficult here. Everyone carries water. It is the way of life.' He blasted his horn as an Indian wandered aimlessly across the road. 'Very stupid people. Sun makes them stupid.' He laughed, showing a

42

mouthful of gold teeth. 'I have a fine schedule for you. *Señora* Vidal will be very pleased.' He glanced slyly at me. '*Señor* Vidal is plenty rich, yes?'

'He has enough,' I said shortly.

'Many poor people live here.' He shook his head sadly. 'Many, many. Rich too. More poor than rich, but rich very rich.'

We were now passing through a small village, crowded with Indians. Most of them wore battered sombreros, white shirts and dark, shapeless trousers. The women had on various coloured aprons, covering their light cotton dresses. The main street of the village was dirty with a litter of paper, discarded fruit skins, cigarette butts and other rubbish. The sight of this squalor depressed me.

It took us over half an hour to reach San Salvador, the capital of El Salvador. It was also swarming with Indians who mingled with well dressed, over-fed men and women, obviously the wealthy citizens of the City.

'Lovely city,' Rivera said. 'You like it, *Señor* Burden?'

'Oh, sure.'

'You call me Roberto. Everyone calls me Roberto. I am a very well known guide here. Many rich Americans ask for me.'

'That's fine.'

'We approach the hotel.' He drove up a steep hill, turned left and edged into a curved drive. 'Beautiful hotel, *Señor* Burden, the best. Everyone very satisfied.'

The doorman opened the car door and I got out. A porter took my bag.

'You'd better come in, Roberto,' I said. 'I'll look at your schedule. I must report to Mr Vidal.'

Roberto showed me his gold teeth.

'No hurry, *Señor* Burden. *Señor* Vidal and the *señora* are with friends for lunch. José – he works with me – took them to El Cuco. Very lovely place by the sea. They visit *Señor* Guzman who owns many coffee plantations, very rich: beautiful, beautiful house, cost two million dollars. They cannot be back here until 19.00. Plenty of time.'

I looked at my watch. It was just midday.

'Okay, Roberto. I'll have lunch here. Suppose we get together around 15.00.'

'I go home then.' He looked happy. 'Nice home: poor, but nice. My children see little of me. It will be a surprise for them.' He lifted his sombrero, shook hands and climbed into the Mercedes.

After checking in, inspecting my room which was air conditioned and pleasant, I took a shower, changed into an open neck shirt and slacks and went down to the Coffee shop for the best scampi cocktail I have ever eaten.

I took coffee on the terrace, overlooking the big pool. The Salvadoranian children all swam like fish and all made a lot of noise. Their parents, solidly built, sat under sun umbrellas, eating ice cream or drinking beer.

Around 15.00, I went into the lounge to find Rivera waiting for me.

'Fine food, *Señor* Burden. Everything satisfactory? Room beautiful?'

'Everything's fine. Let's look at the schedule.'

We went over it together. It meant little to me, not knowing the country, but Rivera assured me there was nothing of interest he had omitted.

'Very hot in the afternoons. I suggest morning drives, *Señor* Burden. Maybe something in the late afternoon when it is cooler. Good to take a little siesta after lunch,' and he looked hopefully at me.

'That will depend on what Mrs Vidal wants. She may not want a siesta.'

His face fell.

'You explain to her, *Señor* Burden. Very hot and fatiguing in the afternoon.'

'I'll see what she says. You had better be here at 08.30 tomorrow morning. I want the car washed and polished, Roberto. These are V.I.P. That car isn't good enough.'

'The best there is, *Señor* Burden, but I will clean it.' He looked even more gloomy. Getting to his feet, he went on, 'Then tomorrow?'

When he had gone, I went over to the kiosk and bought a map of El Salvador, then going up to my room, I put on swim trunks and went down to the pool. After a swim, I sat in the

44

shade and studied the schedule and the map. Tomorrow, we were to visit the Izcola volcano and return to the hotel for lunch. Nothing was suggested for the afternoons. I would have to discuss the afternoons with Mrs Vidal, I told myself.

Around 18.00, after a final swim, I went to my room, shaved, put on a shirt and tie and a lightweight suit and went down to the bar.

An hour later, as I was on my second Scotch and was trying to get some news of interest out of the *New York Tribune*, Henry Vidal bounced into the bar.

Although I had been prepared by Bill Olson what to expect, I realised as Vidal came bustling towards me that no description of him would ever be adequate.

As Olson had said, Vidal was scarcely four foot ten inches high. He had massive shoulders, the shoulders of a wrestler, his short legs were thick and his feet small. He was wearing an open neck scarlet linen shirt, black trousers so tight they appeared to be painted on him and round his thick waist, a broad white belt with a gold buckle.

He wore his greying hair long to his collar. He was completely bald on the top of his head. His baldness emphasised his massive forehead. His beard, also greying, was wiry and thick, but it was his small, glittering eyes that held my attention. As Olson had said, they were hypnotic eyes, penetrating pale blue windows that revealed arrogance, confidence and power.

I got to my feet as he reached me.

'You are Clay Burden? Of course you are.' His voice was high pitched, almost squeaky. He caught my hand in a bone crushing grip, shook it and discarded it.

The barman was at his side.

'Fruit punch,' Vidal said. 'Be careful with the grenadine. It was too heavy last night.' He turned to me. 'Sit down.' He took a chair opposite. 'What are you drinking? Scotch?' He wrinkled his thick nose. 'I never touch alcohol. Never have. Smoking and drinking ruins a mind for business. You like your work? You must do or you wouldn't do it. I hear you are reliable. That is good. I insist on having reliable people around me.' His squeaky voice rattled around my ears like machine gun bullets. 'Dyer arranged for you to amuse my

45

wife while I am busy. I am sure you can do it. She would come with me. I warned her what to expect, but women are so obstinate once they have made up their minds.' He gave a short barking laugh. 'San Salvador is a filthy hole: badly run, no organisation. The Indians will revolt one of these days. You saw all the filth and poverty on the way from the airport? Of course you did. Disgraceful way to live.'

The barman set down a pint glass full of cracked ice and fruit juices. Vidal drank half the punch at a gulp.

'Better. Still too much grenadine.' He turned to me. 'Mrs Vidal has gone to bed. She says she is tired. I can't understand her. I am never tired. I don't know the meaning of the word. Women always have headaches or they are tired. You married? I can see you are. You look responsible. I have no time for a man who isn't responsible. I am sure your wife gets tired too. They all get tired. It is an excuse.' Again he laughed and finished his drink. 'I must change. I have a business dinner.' He jumped to his feet. As I stood up, slightly dazed, he went on, 'Don't disturb yourself. You know what to do tomorrow? I'm sure you do. There's not much to see in this hole but that's her look out. She would come. Do your best.' He crushed my hand again and bounced out of the bar.

I dropped into my chair, finished my drink and signalled to the barman for a refill. I needed it. Olson had said Vidal was a dynamo: that was an understatement. To have to spend a whole evening with him would have reduced me to a nervous wreck.

I thought of his wife and wondered. Did he treat her as he had treated me? If he did, she must be an extraordinary woman to survive.

A heavily built American tourist wandered into the bar. He looked around, spotted me and came over.

'Mind if I join you?' he said, sitting down and waving to the barman. 'My wife tells me it is a bad habit to drink alone,' and he gave me a cheery wink.

I was glad to have company. We talked of this and that for an hour or so, then he heaved himself to his feet.

'I guess the little lady is dressed by now,' he said. 'See you around, friend,' and nodding he ambled out.

I decided to have dinner, then go to my room with a book.

There didn't seem anything else for me to do. I went to the kiosk and found a lurid covered paperback. As I was paying for it, Henry Vidal came bouncing out of the elevator. He was wearing a black silk suit, white shirt and a sky blue tie. He hurried across the lobby without noticing me and climbed into a waiting Mercedes.

I turned and headed for the Coffee shop.

'*Señor* Burden?'

The hall porter had come from behind his desk.

'Yes?'

'A message. Will you please go to suite seven on the fourth floor. *Señora* Vidal wishes to speak to you.'

I stared at him.

'You mean Mrs Vidal?'

He nodded.

Surprised, I stepped into the elevator and pressed button 4. As the cage ascended, it occurred to me that the evening might turn out better than I had anticipated. I was more than interested to see the kind of woman Vidal had married.

I walked down the corridor and paused outside room 7. I knocked.

'Come in.'

The low voice, for no reason I could think of, set my nerves tingling.

I opened the door and walked into a big, comfortably furnished sitting room that contained so many flowers it looked like a florist's shop.

The tall, dark haired, slim woman in a long white wrap was standing by the window.

Although six years had passed since I last saw her, I knew her immediately. My heart gave a little lurch. She was more beautiful now, more poised, more worldly, but still the woman I had never ceased to love.

'Val!' I stood staring at her. 'It can't be you! Val!'

'At last,' she said. 'Darling Clay.'

She came to me, sliding her arms around my neck, her full breasts hard against my chest, her lovely mouth raised to be kissed.

*   *   *

47

The rising moon sent a pale band of light across the bed. Val lay on her back, her eyes half closed, her hands covering her breasts. I lay by her side, looking at her. I still believed I was dreaming as I had dreamed of her so often during the past long years.

We had both thrown away caution and conscience during the first kiss. We had found ourselves on the bed, naked and straining for each other.

I was aware as I watched her of an almost weightless feeling and being more relaxed than I had ever been, but also aware that my love for her was ever more acute.

She pressed her hands to her face.

'Darling Clay, you don't know how dangerous this is,' she whispered. 'We shouldn't have done it. I should have kept away from you. I planned it all. You can't imagine the trouble I've had. When I heard you had come to Paradise City, I couldn't resist seeing you. There is so much to talk about.' She turned her head swiftly and looked at the bedside clock. 'But not now. Get dressed. We have five days in which to talk.'

The time was 20.40.

'Let's talk now,' I said. I longed to hear what had been happening to her during the past six years. 'It's early still.'

'No! Get dressed!' The urgency in her voice made me reach for my clothes. 'You don't know what he is like. If he ever even suspected what has happened, he would ruin you. He is so vindictive and vicious and there's nothing he can't do once he has set his mind to it. He would keep after you so you would never be able to work again. I mean it, Clay. You must believe me.'

Shocked, I stared at her.

'Be careful when you leave,' she went on. 'Make sure there's no one outside.'

I was dressed now. As I bent to kiss her, she pushed me away.

'No . . . please go! We'll talk tomorrow.'

'When tomorrow?' The panic in her eyes made me uneasy.

'When he goes. I don't know. Wait for me in the lobby. As soon as he goes.'

'Oh, Val . . . I can't believe this has happened. I . . .'

'Please go! Suppose he walked in . . . ' She shivered.

I went to the sitting room door, opened it silently and peered out into the long corridor, then drew hurriedly back as I saw a man and a woman moving towards the elevators.

'What is it?' She had come to the bedroom door, still naked. Her whisper was loaded with fear.

I raised my hand to silence her, then peered out again, aware that my heart was now thumping. Her fear had communicated itself to me. The couple entered the elevator. Without looking back, I moved into the corridor as the elevator doors slid shut. I walked quickly down the corridor to the stairs and down them to the third floor and to my room.

I went immediately to the bathroom and stared at myself in the mirror. There was a smudge of lipstick by my mouth. I stared at my pale, excited face. There was a different look about me that was hard to define. Could it be I now looked younger and was that guilty fear in my eyes?

I ran cold water and bathed my face, then going into the bedroom, I opened the french windows and stepped out on to the balcony.

The night air was hot and humid. The big moon rose high above the distant city lights. I could hear the soft strains of the dance band and somewhere under the palms, a girl laughed.

With unsteady hands, I took out my pack of cigarettes and sat down in the lounging chair. I lit the cigarette and stared up at the moon.

Now drained of desire and alerted by Val's warning, I realised that I had been crazy to have given way to that overpowering sexual urge. Val had been crazy too. Both of us were to blame. We had completely lost control of ourselves.

I remembered what she had said. *You don't know what he is like. If he found out, he would ruin you. He is so vindictive and vicious.* It had been the frightened tone of her voice more than her words that sent a chill up my spine. I knew from past experience that Val wasn't easily frightened. I had seen enough of Vidal to know she hadn't been talking heedlessly nor as an alarmist. Those arrogant, confident eyes told me as nothing else could that if he ever found out about us, he would exact a vicious revenge.

Then my mind switched to Rhoda. If she ever found out! I was sure she would be nearly as vindictive as Vidal. She would never forgive me for preferring another woman.

My conscience was now tormenting me. I thought of tomorrow. Should I make an excuse, say I was ill, say anything to avoid spending the next five days with Val, knowing the danger of giving myself away when with her to some sharp eyed onlooker? Could I spend whole days with her with Rivera at the wheel without alerting his suspicions that she had taken me as her lover?

I pulled myself together.

This was stupid, panicky thinking. It had happened and it mustn't happen again. It had been, I told myself, an explosive madness and it was now over. But even as I told myself this, even after loving her but an hour ago and drained of desire, I knew it wasn't and couldn't be over. No matter how great the risk, if she wanted me, I knew I wouldn't and couldn't resist her.

So I sat on the balcony, unaware of the passing hours, thinking of her.

Val! Married to Vidal! It was unbelievable. How had they met? Then I remembered Olson had told me that Vidal was once a client of his. Maybe she had met Vidal when she had been working with Olson.

But why had she married this balding dwarf? According to Olson, at that time, Vidal was far from rich. She couldn't have married him for his money. Then what had induced her to prefer him to me?

That was something that disconcerted and hurt me far more than finding her tied to this now wealthy tycoon and so obviously frightened of him.

I took these thoughts to bed with me. I scarcely slept and when the waiter brought me coffee at 07.30 I was glad to get up.

I went down to the lobby at 08.30. The hall porter bowed to me.

'Roberto is waiting, *señor*,' he said.

'I'll have a word with him.' I paused, then asked, 'Is Mr Vidal in the hotel?'

'*Señor* Vidal left at eight.'

I went out to where Rivera was lounging in the shade. He came over to me, smiling, his gold teeth flashing in the sun.

'Good morning, *Señor* Burden. Beautiful morning. You had a fine night?'

'Thank you. Where is the car?'

He pointed. I went over and inspected it. He had had it cleaned and it now looked reasonably presentable.

'Much hard work,' Rivera said mournfully. 'Very big car.'

'I'll see if Mrs Vidal is ready.'

Returning to the lobby, I picked up one of the telephones and asked to be connected to suite 7.

Val came on the line almost immediately. The sound of her voice again made my nerves tingle.

'Good morning, Mrs Vidal,' I said, aware the hall porter was listening. 'The car is waiting. We can leave whenever you are ready.'

'Thank you. I will be down in a few minutes.'

I hung up and wandered over to the kiosk where I bought a pack of cigarettes.

Val appeared from the elevator ten minutes later. She was wearing a blue and white flowered shirt, white stretch pants and her hair was caught back with a white bandeau. She looked breathlessly beautiful.

'Good morning, Mr Burden,' she said brightly. Her eyes were impersonal and her smile remote. 'Where are we going this morning?'

'Would you step over here for a moment, please? I would like to show you the schedule.'

I moved to an isolated settee and she followed me. We sat down, out of ear-shot of the hall porter and the reception desk.

As I took the schedule from my pocket, I said, keeping my voice low, 'There's a complication, Val. We have a chauffeur. It's my own damn fault. I didn't know it would be you. It would be dangerous to get rid of him. He might talk.'

I saw the disappointment in her eyes, but she kept her face expressionless as she said, 'So what do we do?'

'He doesn't want to work in the afternoons. He says it would be too hot. We could meet in my room after lunch. I must talk to you, Val!'

She thought about this, then she nodded.

'All right. Let's go now. Where are we going?'

'To see the Izalco volcano. He'll tell you about it. I'll sit up front with him. Be careful, Val. He's a Maya and no fool. Don't make any slips.'

Together, we went out into the sunshine. Seeing us come Rivera scrambled out of the car and opened the rear door, sweeping off his sombrero as he did so.

'Good morning, *señora*. A beautiful day. We go on a beautiful excursion. Very, very interesting. I tell you the history as we go.'

Val thanked him and got in the car. I went around and got in beside Rivera.

I don't think either Val nor I heard more than a few words of Rivera's drone. All I could think of was the coming afternoon when we would be alone together. The drive to the volcano was long, dusty and tortuous. Parts of the road were so bad we had to crawl.

Eventually we arrived at Hotel de Montana which stands empty but from which, Rivera assured us, we would have a fine view of the crater. At any other time, the perfect shaped cone, dark grey in colour, would have been an impressive sight to me, but my mind was too occupied with the thought of the coming afternoon to be anything but impatient as Rivera praised its magnificence. He was sharp enough to see that neither Val nor I were showing sufficient interest.

'You don't like?' he asked, looking searchingly at Val. 'You are not satisfied, *Señora* Vidal?'

'I think it is perfectly marvellous, but it is hotter than I thought. Let us return to the hotel.'

His little eyes brightened.

'Midday too hot. After lunch, it would be wise to take a siesta. The evening will be cooler. If you wish, *señora*, I drive you around the city in the evening.'

'I think this will be enough for today. We will see the city tomorrow.'

He positively beamed.

'Very wise. Better to swim in beautiful pool. Then we go back now?'

'Yes, please.'

We reached the hotel a little after 13.00. Val thanked Rivera for his careful driving and for showing her the volcano.

Leaving him, we entered the lobby.

'Let us have a light lunch together, Mr Burden,' Val said. 'Then I'll take a siesta.' This was for the benefit of the hall porter who was bowing to her.

We went into the crowded Coffee shop and had a hamburger each. I left half mine and we scarcely exchanged a word.

As we were leaving, I said, 'Don't hand in your key, Val.' She nodded.

'Third floor. Room 346,' and screening the move with my body, I gave her my key.

Smiling at me, she went across to the elevators. I walked to the far end of the lobby, lit a cigarette and sat down. After a ten minute wait, I got casually to my feet and took the elevator to the 3rd floor.

Val was lying on my bed, naked.

I hurriedly shut and locked the door.

'Val! We mustn't. We . . .'

She held out her arms. The flush on her face and the brightness of her eyes swept away all caution. I threw off my clothes and joined her.

This time our love making was without the violent urgency of the previous night. This time we were gentle with each other, letting the climax build slowly until we reached the crest, then, together, we surged down the long lane of light, swiftly and silently, feeling the world blotted out in the moment of ecstasy that left us breathless.

*   *   *

In the air conditioned room, with the sun blinds drawn against the heat of the afternoon, Val, lying by my side on the bed, told me something of the six years she had spent with Henry Vidal.

53

She puzzled me by saying that she wasn't expecting me to understand everything she was going to tell me and I would have to be patient with her. It would be difficult, she said, for her to explain why she had written that letter and why she had returned the ring, but in fairness to us both, she had to try.

'To begin at the beginning,' she said, 'I first met him when he came to the office at the Statler-Hilton. Bill Olson was at lunch. I was on my own. He wanted a flight to London. While I was checking the flight and preparing the ticket, I was aware that he was staring at me so intensely that he embarrassed me. It was the busy season and I kept being interrupted by telephone calls. I apologised for keeping him waiting, but he said he was in no hurry. I've often thought about that first meeting. I believed then and I know now that he was trying to hypnotise me. While he was with me I felt some tremendous energy and dynamic power stifling me. Does that sound nonsense to you? I assure you that was how I felt. He paid for the ticket and still staring at me, he said he would see me again. I kept thinking of him. It was as if he had taken hold of part of my mind.' She made a helpless little gesture. 'I began to dream about him. I kept imagining he was following me. I became nervy and I ceased to go out once I was back home from the office, but that didn't stop the dreams.' She touched my wrist. 'The dreadful thing about this was that I no longer thought of you, but always of him. Your letters arrived so faithfully. Some I didn't even read. I know this will hurt you, but you must try to understand that at that time I was fighting desperately not to be possessed. Evil spirits do try to possess people.' She looked fixedly at me. 'Do you believe that, Clay?'

I had never thought about evil spirits. To me, Vidal was just an arrogant, self-opinionated tycoon.

'I don't know, but go on. What happened?' I said.

'When he returned from London he came to the office nearly every day on some pretext or other. I even changed lunch hours with Bill so I could avoid him, but it made no difference. But why go on? I fought him for two dreadful months, but he was too much for me. I finally gave up and he took possession of me.'

54

'Are you telling me that he forced you to marry him?' I asked, staring at her.

'He didn't force me. He took possession of me. I knew that unless I submitted to him, I would never have any peace nor rest again. I was so tired and so frightened. It was easier to marry him than to continue the struggle.'

'But why didn't you tell me what was happening? I would have come back and helped you.'

'No one could help me. When you are faced with that kind of struggle you either save yourself or you go under. This was a personal battle which I lost. Besides, Clay, I loved you as I love you still. I knew he would sweep you away if you tried to interfere. You would have had no weapon against his power. I did think of telling you, then I thought, Why spoil two lives? I told myself I wasn't worth putting you in danger. So I wrote to you and returned your ring.'

I looked at her, baffled. How could anyone be expected to believe this rigmarole?

'You still don't understand, do you, Clay? He is evil! He is a devil! You don't believe in devils, do you?'

Her fear and the wildness in her eyes alarmed me.

'Surely devils went out in the last century,' I said. 'No. I don't believe in devils nor evil spirits, but I can understand a man of his energy and power sweeping you off your feet. I grant you he is dynamic, but this talk about being hypnotised, possessed . . . about spirits . . . no. I can't go along with mumbo jumbo like that.'

She nodded as if telling herself this was what she expected me to say.

'All right, Clay, let us say he swept me off my feet. Let us agree about that. It is much less complicated, although it is not fair to me. Never mind. Don't let's waste time. I once asked him why he married me. I remember his exact words: "I am going to be rich," he said, staring at me with those frightening eyes. "Money is power and I want power. You are going to help me. I have chosen you as my partner because you have a quick, intelligent mind and you are thoroughly efficient. You also have looks. The moment I saw you I knew you were the ideal woman I was looking for. Together, we will work and achieve." ' She stared up at the ceiling, her eyes cloudy. 'In four years, with me by his side, he has become what he is. He has unlimited power and unlimited money. There is in him a ruthless evil drive that won't ever let him stop. He will go on amassing money and power until he dies. A year after I married him, he made his first million. It didn't even give him pleasure, let alone satisfaction. "This is just the beginning," he said. "This is nothing!" How we worked! We never stopped travelling, meeting people, bribing people. How I hated it! But I was a Trilby to his Svengali. He told me what to do, I did it.'

There was a long pause while she continued to stare up at the ceiling.

'And now . . . after six years?' I was depressed. I couldn't accept this extraordinary story. Trilby and Svengali! (What did she mean?) Spirits. Devils. I would much rather she told me that she had fallen madly in love with Vidal and now that love had turned sour. I could have accepted that but not this nonsense about being possessed and hypnotised.

'My life is becoming my own again,' she said. 'He has less use for me. I have become redundant. He is too busy to entertain much, but when he does, then I have to arrange everything. He spends weeks locked in his office. He has many people working for him. For a year now he hasn't told me what he is doing, what he is planning. He likes to have me around. I am an ornament . . . nothing else. He doesn't need my help any more and I am thankful. I have leisure now. This has given me time to think, and my thoughts, Clay, have been of you. You don't know how I have regretted sending your ring back, but please try to understand, at that time, I was half out of my mind. Even when life was most hectic and we were rushing from one city to another, one country to another, I found time to think of you. Then last month I saw in the papers that A.T.S. were opening at the Spanish Bay hotel and you were to be in charge. I went to Dyer. He is nervous of me. He isn't sure if I have influence or not. He knows I once worked for the A.T.S. It wasn't difficult to persuade him to transfer the account to you. I said I wanted to do my old firm a favour. He accepted that, and made no difficulty about the change. Then when I heard Henry was going on a business trip here, I persuaded him to let me come with him. I hadn't been on a trip with him for some time. I said I wanted a change, that I would have a guide and see the country while he worked. I told Dyer you were to be the guide.' She patted my hand. 'You resisted, didn't you? I got my way in the end and here we are.' She rolled towards me, sliding her arms around me. 'Forgive me for hurting you, darling, and do try to understand how it happened.'

I gently stroked her hip.

'Although I have never forgotten you, Val, I really believed I had lost you for good. You know I'm married?'

She nodded.

'Dyer told me. Does she make you happy, Clay?'

'We are married.'

'I've been honest with you, Clay, please be honest with me. Does she make you happy?'

'No. We get along. We have really nothing in common. You've met her. She works at The Trendie Miss.'

'Rhoda? Is she your wife?'

'Yes.'

'But she's pretty and so gay. Have you been married long, Clay?'

'Two years. It was a mistake.'

She looked searchingly at me.

'You don't love her?'

'I love you.'

She rested her face against mine.

'You don't know how good it is to hear you say that. I don't think I can live without you now, Clay.'

'I thought about you all last night. I can't bear the thought of losing you again. What can we do? Would he divorce you?'

I felt her stiffen.

'No! I wouldn't dare even ask him. If he thought I wanted to leave him for you, God knows what he would do!'

'But what can he do?' I said impatiently. 'Tell him you love me and I'll tell Rhoda I love you. They must give us a divorce.'

'Clay! I told you he is evil. I told you he is a devil. He has thugs working for him. He has only to give them instructions and they follow out those instructions. A man once tried

to cheat him. That man was attacked by these thugs. He is
going about in a wheelchair now. He is half an idiot.'

I stared at her.

'Didn't the police . . . ?'

'A dark night, a vicious blow . . . what can the police do?
If he found out we are lovers he would turn his thugs loose
on you and on me. There was a stupid, greedy girl who tried
to threaten him with a paternity case. She hoped to get
money out of him. She was crazy. One of his thugs threw acid
in her face. She is now blind.'

Fear laid cold hands on me.

'So when I said God knows what he would do to you and
to me if I asked him for a divorce I'm stating a fact. He might
even have us killed.'

'I can't believe . . .'

'I'm telling you!' Her voice became shrill. She half sat up,
glaring at me, the fear in her eyes was chilling. 'He'll have us
killed!'

Her fear was so real, I could only stare helplessly at her.

'Does that mean . . .'

'There is a way. I've been thinking and thinking for the
past week and I have found a solution that would be safe.
Always providing you really don't want to be parted from
me as I can't bear the thought of being parted from you. It is
a solution that won't even interfere with your marriage.'

'What is it?'

'I will persuade him to employ you to look after his travel
affairs. You would be like Dyer, a member of the staff. You
would have an office in the house. When he is away, there
would be no danger.' She looked questioningly at me. 'What
do you think?'

I shook my head doubtfully.

'Why should he be persuaded?'

'He would agree for two reasons. He would save agency
fees and I would be occupied. He is continually telling me to
find something to do. You see, darling, we would work
together, I would again be your secretary,' She gripped my
arm, her eyes shining. 'Of course we would have to be careful,
but we would have moments like this again when he goes
away.'

58

I was still doubtful, but I could see the possibility of such a plan.

'But what about Dyer?'

'He is overworked as it is. He would be glad to be rid of the travel business. There would be no problem with him.'

I was beginning to get excited.

'It sounds too good to be true!'

'It's better than that. What are you earning now?'

I told her.

'He would pay you twice as much and even then save money. You would work office hours. You would return home as you always do.' She brushed my cheek with her lips. 'Neither he nor Rhoda would ever know.'

And stupidly, I believed her.

Four

THE NEXT four days followed a pattern. Every morning we set off sight-seeing with Rivera. It was irritating that we had to be separated in the car, but we both agreed that it would be unwise to sit together. A change like that might make Rivera suspicious.

We toured the city and visited the Mercado central which was swarming with Indians: their multi-coloured produce – black beans, water melons, yellow corn, scarlet tomatoes and pink, sticky cakes – making an exotic carpet on the dusty, litter strewn street. Rivera drove us to Acajalta to see the Port where liners from Panama disgorge tourists into waiting buses for a brief glimpse of the city. We visited a coffee *beneficio* where we watched the turning of the red berries into *café de oro*, the final drying out of the bean before sacking. He took us to the village of Ilobasco where elderly craftsmen made microscopic dolls of clay: a dying art, Rivera told us sadly. 'The young have no patience for such exact work.'

Each day we returned to the hotel in time for a light lunch. Then Val joined me in my room. From time to time I caught a brief glimpse of Vidal as he hurried into or out of the elevator. He gave me the impression of a man trying to cram thirty-six hours into twenty-four hours and just succeeding.

I had the evening to myself. Val and Vidal, with business associates did the night club rounds: a chore, Val told me, that drove her nearly crazy with boredom. During the evenings, after a solitary dinner, I took long walks around the city. I was free to think over Val's proposed plan. Providing Vidal agreed, it seemed to me to be a solution, although not a lasting nor entirely satisfactory one. But after some thought, I decided it was certainly better than nothing. As Val seemed sure that we ran no risk of detection, I was prepared to be convinced too. I wondered what Massingham would say when I told him I was leaving the firm to work for Vidal. Would he think it unethical? Could he make difficulties for me? Val had said she would persuade Vidal to give me a three year contract. If she succeeded, then I needn't worry about Massingham's reaction. How would Rhoda react? I would have to compensate her by giving her extra money for her lunches and buy her a small car so she could get to and fro now she wouldn't have me to drive her. I doubted if she would give a damn one way or the other.

Val had warned me that I must have patience.

'I have to catch him in the right mood and when he is less busy,' she said, as we lay on the bed together. 'I'll watch for my chance as soon as we get back.'

Although I thought often of her claim to be possessed by Vidal, I didn't broach the subject with her again. She seemed willing to accept my disbelief and I dismissed the spirits and the devils as an hysterical phase that was, I hoped, now in the past.

Then something happened that made me wonder if, perhaps, she hadn't been exaggerating.

On our last afternoon at the hotel, we had made love and were lying side by side on the bed in my room. Val's hand rested lightly on my arm. I was completely relaxed and drowsy. Every now and then the thought that tomorrow we would be leaving San Salvador kept edging into my mind. The past days had a dream-like quality. Although San Salvador had been disappointing as a city, it would still remain a shrine to me of the four most wonderful days in my life. Tomorrow I would be back to face Rhoda's careless sluttishness. I wondered in what mess I would find the apartment. The cleaning woman didn't come in on Saturdays or Sundays. It was my job to keep the place reasonably decent over the week-ends. I was fully expecting to return to chaos, but I was too relaxed and happy to give this more than a moment's thought.

Then suddenly without warning, Val's fingers gripped my

arm so violently, her nails cutting into my flesh, that I gave
an involuntary cry.

'Val! What is it?'

I jerked my arm free and stared at her.

There was an expression of terror in her eyes that frightened me. She had turned pale, her lips were trembling and I
could see she was shivering.

'Val!'

She scrambled off the bed, and with desperate haste, began
pulling on her stretch pants.

'He's here!' she gasped. 'He's come back! I always know!
I get this awful pain when he is near!' She dragged her shirt
over her head, thrust her feet into her sandals, then ran over
to the mirror.

'He can't be here!' I said, but her panic was infectious. I
too began to throw on my clothes. 'It's not four o'clock.
Rivera told me he wouldn't be back until eight.'

'He's here!' She dragged my comb through her hair, then
paused, bending double, her hands pressed to her sides. 'God!
It hurts!'

I was dressed now.

'Stop being hysterical!' I exclaimed, angry that she was
frightening me. 'He can't be here! Sit down! You have a
cramp!'

'He's here I tell you!' She moaned, pressing her sides. 'Go
down! Stall him until I get to my room. Quick!'

The panic in her voice flustered me. With by heart thumping, I left the room, ran to the elevator and pressed the call
button. As I stood waiting, I told myself she was dramatising
a situation that didn't exist. Rivera had told me that Vidal
had gone to Santa Rosa de Lima to visit the owner of a sugar
plantation. Rivera had been gloomy. 'It is a very long, hot
drive, *Señor* Burden,' he had said. 'Poor José! He will miss
his siesta. He won't be back before eight.'

As the elevator door swished open and I moved into the
lobby, I saw Henry Vidal. He was standing by the reception
desk, collecting a thick packet of mail.

The sight of him gave me such a jolt, I stood rooted, a cold
sick sensation developing in the pit of my stomach.

As if sensing my presence, he turned abruptly. Then he

came towards me, his short, thick legs taking bouncing strides.

'How is the sight-seeing?' he demanded in his squeaky voice. His hard little eyes searched my face. 'Nothing much I am sure. Well, she would come. I warned her. Women are obstinate. No sight-seeing this afternoon? Too hot for her, I suppose. She wilts in the heat. It's never too hot for me. I thrive on it. She is in her room, resting, of course, when she should be exercising in the pool. She hasn't enough to do.' He began to flick through the envelopes. I tried to think of something to say, but my mind was a panic-stricken blank. 'We leave tomorrow.' His little eyes lifted to my face, then back to the envelopes. 'We will be down here at 07.45. Handle everything, Mr Burden. Tips . . . baggage . . . I don't have to tell you.' He looked up. 'Accept two hundred dollars for your service. My wife tells me you have been most helpful. Thank you,' and moving around me, he entered the elevator and was whisked out of sight.

Val would be back in the suite by now. Would she give herself away? I thought not. It had been a narrow escape . . . too narrow.

There were a few people around the pool. A number of small children splashed and yelled. I went down the steps and into the sunshine and walking as far from the pool as I could get, I sat down under a sun umbrella.

My mind was crawling with alarm. How had Val known Vidal had returned? Could she be psychic? I recalled how her face had been contorted with pain as she had pressed her hands to her body. *I get this awful pain when he is near.* I had read about mediums and spirit sessions in the newspapers but I had dismissed these odd people either as fakes or cranks. I was sure Val wasn't a crank.

Possessed?

When at school I had studied the Bible. Now I remember reading of people being possessed of the devil. Val had said Vidal was a devil.

I recalled what she had said: *Evil spirits do try to possess people. He is evil! He is a devil!*

I now wanted to question her and to listen, without scoffing, to her answers. But I would have no opportunity to talk to her until we returned to Paradise City. Then another thought occurred to me: a thought that turned my mouth dry. Was Vidal suspicious of her and of me?

I got up and walked around the back of the hotel to where the waiting taxis were parked. There was just a chance that José, Vidal's driver, was still hanging around, but, of course, he wasn't. As I was re-entering the hotel, I spotted Rivera lounging in the shade, talking to one of the hotel porters. I moved towards him and he, seeing me approaching, got to his feet and joined me.

'The last day here, *Señor* Burden. Very sad for me. The *señora* perhaps would like a nice drive when it is cooler?'

'I don't think so.' I was surprised he made the offer until I remembered he was thinking of his tip. 'Mr Vidal returned unexpectedly. I doubt if she will be going out.'

He beamed.

'It was very fortunate for José. He did not have to drive to Santa Rosa de Lima. *Señor* Vidal's friend met him half-way at Zacatecoluca because of the heat.'

So that was it.

I drew in a breath of relief. Vidal hadn't been suspicious of us. This hadn't been a manoeuvre to catch us in the act.

'Will you have the car ready tomorrow at 07.30?' I said.

'Yes, *Señor* Burden. You can rely on me.' He paused and looked hopefully at me. 'If the *señora* doesn't need me, I go.'

'I'll check first.'

I went into the lobby and called suite 7. Val answered.

'This is Burden,' I said. 'Roberto wants to know if you would like a last drive?'

'I'll ask my husband.' Her voice sounded calm. There was a pause, then she said, 'No, it is all right. We are going to take a swim later,' and she hung up.

I told Rivera he could go and he went off happily. The time was 17.10. I had nothing to do. I would have liked to have taken a swim but if Val and Vidal were coming down I thought it wiser to keep out of their way.

So I walked down to the city and in the stifling heat, wandered around the shops. I suddenly remembered I should take Rhoda back a present: no easy task as she was always critical of what I bought her. I finally bought a snake skin

64

belt which I thought might please her.

I returned to the hotel at 18.30 and went to the bar. Carrying a gin and tonic out on to the terrace, I sat down.

As I settled myself, I looked across the pool. Val and Vidal were sitting under the shade of a tree. He was wearing purple swim trunks. His chunky body was covered with coarse black hair. Looking at him, I saw the brutal power and strength of him. With his short thick legs and his barrel shaped chest he looked more like an ape than a human being.

Abruptly, he turned his head and looked at me. He seemed to feel instinctively if anyone was regarding him. Then he spoke to Val, looking beautiful in an emerald green bikini. She looked in my direction and smiled, then nodded to Vidal who raised his hand and beckoned to me to join them.

*   *   *

The San Salvador–Guatemala–Miami flight was full. Arriving at el Aeropuerto de Ilpango twenty minutes before take-off, Vidal said to me, 'Call us when we can board,' and he and Val went to the V.I.P. lounge.

Rivera and I checked in the luggage. I got hold of one of the air hostesses and warned her the Vidals were on her flight. She promised to take care of them. I then tipped Rivera, shook hands with him and thanked him for his service, not that he deserved thanking. He had done as little as possible.

When the last of the passengers had passed through the security screen, I went to the V.I.P. lounge.

'All ready for boarding, Mr Vidal,' I said.

They took their seats. Satisfied they were in good hands – already the air hostess was offering them champagne which they refused – I went to the economy class and took my seat.

In one week from tomorrow I would be a member of Vidal's staff. I still couldn't believe it. Val had promised she would catch Vidal in the right mood and she had seized the chance when he had returned so unexpectedly. This surprised me. I had left her terrified, yet she had been able to recover enough to persuade Vidal he would save money by employing me.

When I joined them by the pool, Val had said she would

change for dinner and she left Vidal and me together.

'This idea my wife has of you joining my staff,' he said as soon as she had gone, 'is smart. Dyer should have thought of it. It will save me money.' He gave me a sharp look. 'Save the dimes, Burden' (I noted the 'mister' had been dropped), 'and the dollars take care of themselves. I should have been told agency commissions were so high. She tells me she has discussed the idea with you and you're ready to work for me. That's okay with me. I'll give you a week to tie up your end, so report to Dyer tomorrow week, huh? My wife wants to work with you. That's constructive thinking. She knows the work and it will occupy her. Everyone needs to be occupied. She tells me you are efficient. I hope so, Burden. I don't get along with inefficiency. See my attorney, Jason Shackman. He will give you a contract. You will take instructions from my wife. If you have any questions, ask her.' He got to his feet. 'Keep on your toes. Pull your weight and you'll be happy working with us.' He bounced away to the hotel.

I leaned back in my seat and fastened the safety belt. It had come off! In a week's time I would once again be working with Val. It would be turning the clock back six years. To be with her constantly was my greatest wish. *There will be moments like this when he is away*, she had promised. Those were the moments I would live for.

I thought of all the things I had to do during the coming week. I thought of Rhoda. I would have to be very careful not to give her the slightest suspicion there was more to this offer of Vidal's than promotion and money.

I must warn Val to keep away from the Trendie Miss boutique. It would be fatal if Olson saw her. He might tell Rhoda who she was and then the red light would go up.

At Miami airport, I joined Val and Vidal at the Customs' barrier.

'Take care of the baggage, Burden,' Vidal said abruptly. 'Come, Valerie. The Rolls will be waiting.'

There was some delay before I cleared the baggage, then, as I followed the porter out into the lobby, I saw Vernon Dyer, immaculate in a lemon coloured suit, waiting. He gave me a sneering little grin.

'So you have become one of us, you poor, misguided

fellow,' he said. 'Tiny has just broken the news to me.'

'Tiny?'

'We call him that: top secret of course. Well, welcome to the slave house. I hear our Mrs V. is putting her harness on again. At least, Tiny won't have to pay her, but rather you than me. Strictly between slaves, old boy, she can be difficult: repeat difficult. There are times when she can even be horrid.' He chuckled. 'Must be frustration. It can't be fun to bed with hairy Tiny.'

I felt like hitting him, but I controlled myself.

'I've got baggage here.'

'I'll take care of it. Thank God this is the last time I'll have to be his dreary porter. See you next Monday, old boy,' and with a languid wave of his hand, he directed the bagman to take the baggage to a waiting estate wagon.

Back home, I found the expected chaos. Surprisingly, Rhoda was out. The bedroom and the living room were in a depressing state of confusion. She had managed to spill her face powder over her dressing table. Cigarette butts overflowed from ash trays. The bed was unmade. She had dropped her lipstick on the carpet and had trodden on it. The bathroom was in a complete mess and her clothes lay where she had dropped them. I spent a couple of hours clearing up. By then it was lunch time. I made myself a martini and went into the kitchen. As I expected she had done no shopping for the week-end. Apart from a few cans of sardines, there was nothing to eat.

I wondered where she had got to. We seldom went out on Sundays. She preferred to slop around and sunbathe on the balcony. I had had only a cup of coffee on the aircraft and I was now hungry. I decided to go down to the Coffee shop. As I started towards the door, Rhoda came in.

'Oh, hello.' She came across to peck me on the cheek. 'I wasn't sure when you would be back. Have a good trip?'

For a Sunday she looked surprisingly smart although she hadn't bothered to put on her usual elaborate make-up.

'Where have you been?' I asked.

'At the Club.' She pouted. 'I got bored sticking around here on my own. Is there anything to eat?'

'You know there isn't! Let's go to the Coffee shop.'

'Oh, God! That again! I thought you might have picked something up on your way back.'

'Well, I didn't. I've got something for you.' I gave her the snake skin belt.

She promptly found fault with it.

'It's not my size and what am I going to wear with it?'

'That's your problem. Come on . . . I'm hungry.'

We went down to the Coffee shop and ordered steaks.

'How did you get on with the slinky Mrs Vidal?' she asked, once the order was given. She looked at me with a jeering little grin. 'Have you fallen for her?'

I reached for a roll and began to butter it.

'Sorry to disappoint you. There is no romance in the offing.'

'Well, at least, admit she isn't bad looking.'

'I admit she isn't bad looking.'

I could see she was irritated I wasn't rising to the bait. 'You mean she didn't try to drag you into her bed?'

'Shall we skip this drivel, honey,' I said quietly. 'I've something important to tell you, but if you must play your not so funny game, I'll wait until you are through.' I thought this was the safest way to play it. I was right. She flushed angrily. She hated to be treated like a child.

'So what's so important?' she demanded.

'Are you quite sure you don't want to continue about Mrs Vidal?'

'Cut it out, Clay! Don't be so filthy! What's important?'

'I'm changing my job. Vidal made me an offer to come on his staff and I've accepted it.'

Her eyes popped open wide.

'You mean you're leaving A.T.S.?'

'That's right.'

'But why?'

'The money is twice as good as I'm getting now and the work will be much more interesting. It's an opportunity too good to miss.'

'Is it?' She paused as the waitress set the plates before us. 'How about your pension? You've worked for A.T.S. for years. I think you are nuts. Suppose Vidal drops dead? What will you do then?'

These were shrewd points which I hadn't considered. I couldn't tell her the reason I was going to work for Vidal and the only reason was that I would be in continual contact with Val.

'He won't drop dead and he's taking care of the pension angle.'

She ate some of the steak, frowning.

'Well, I suppose you know what you are doing. Where will you work?'

'He has offices close to the house.'

'Hey! What about me?' She put down her knife and fork and stared at me. 'How do I get to work and home again?'

'With the extra money he is paying I can afford to buy a car for you.'

Her eyes lit up.

'Honest?'

'That's what the man said.'

'I don't want some crummy heap, Clay. I want either an Austin Cooper or a Toyota.'

'You can have what you want.'

'Big deal, huh?' I could see she was pleased. She was so busy thinking about the car, she raised no further objections. It was as easy as that. However, while we were getting ready for bed after watching TV, she said suddenly, 'I suppose you'll be seeing a lot of Slinky?'

'Who?'

'Mrs Vidal.'

'I doubt it. From what I hear she travels a lot with Vidal.'

'Oh.' Rhoda thought for a moment, then decided not to pursue the subject. 'Come on to bed. I feel sexy.'

I didn't but this wasn't the time to say no. When I put out the light and took her in my arms, I thought of Val, but even thinking of her wasn't enough to turn me on.

When it was over, Rhoda said crossly, 'What's the matter with you? That was a complete drag.'

'Sorry. I have a lot on my mind.'

'You can say that again,' and she turned her back to me.

I lay in the darkness, thinking of Val. It was long past midnight before I fell asleep.

*   *   *

The following week proved a busy one and I was glad to have Olson to handle the routine work. I saw Massingham and told him of Vidal's offer.

He took it well.

'It's up to you, Clay,' he said. 'We'll be sorry to lose you. Are you sure you're doing the right thing? Vidal could be here today, gone tomorrow.'

'Oh, I wouldn't say that. I've thought about it. I need a change. There will be more to it than booking tickets and the money is good.'

'All right. Try it. See how you like working for him. If it doesn't work out, come back to us. There'll always be a place for you.'

It was more than I had expected.

I called on Vidal's attorney, Jason Shackman. He had my contract ready. It was a simple affair. Either party could give six months' notice: the contract to run for three years with a salary increase each year. I signed. He signed, and that was that.

Rhoda had her Austin Cooper and loved it. Although I was busy, the days dragged. I longed for the moment when I would see Val again.

On Saturday morning, as I was clearing my desk, Dyer came in.

'All fixed for Monday, old boy?' he asked. 'I've been saving it all up for you. You'll be as busy as a buzz saw. Tiny is going on a trip at the end of the week. Bring plenty of tranquillisers with you.' He took a blue card in a plastic envelope from his pocket. 'This is your pass. Show it to the guard at the barrier. Don't lose it.' He looked around my office, then rested a hip on my desk. 'It foxes me why you're giving this up. Here, you are your own boss and you have fixed hours of work.' He shrugged. 'It's your funeral. You'll appreciate this after a week or so working for Tiny.' He looked thoughtfully at me. 'Take a tip from me and be careful of Mrs V. Strictly between you and me, she's an odd ball. There are times when she really baffles me. She's fine one day, then moody and far away the next. The damnedest thing happened a couple of months ago. She and I were discussing the arrangements for a big dinner party. I couldn't remember the name of one of

70

the guests. She couldn't either. Then just when we were about to give up, I remembered. I snapped my fingers like this.' With thumb and third finger, he made a loud snapping noise. 'Believe it or not, she went into a trance. You know . . . like a subject who has been hypnotised. She just sat motionless, her eyes empty: she looked like a goddamn zombie. Gave me a hell of a turn. I had seen the trick done at a night club. I snapped my fingers twice in her face and she came to as fast as she had gone into the trance. She didn't seem to know what had happened.' He took out his gold cigarette case and offered it. 'Odd, don't you think?'

I refused the cigarette. It was as much as I could do to keep my face expressionless.

As I said nothing, he scowled. That I appeared to show no interest in what he had told me plainly irritated him.

'Well, don't say you haven't been warned,' he went on. 'No finger snapping, old boy, unless, of course, you want to make her your slave, but with Tiny around that would be most unwise.'

'You'll have to excuse me,' I said curtly. 'I'm trying to clear up,' and opening a desk drawer I began to empty it.

'Mustn't hold you up gossiping then.' He slid off my desk. 'Have a nice week-end.' He moved to the door, then paused. 'Oh, one other thing. Tiny works seven days a week. Don't count on your future week-ends. I never do,' and on that cheerful note, he left.

I had no time to think over what he had told me about Val as Olson came in with some last minute queries. We were all kept busy until 13.00. Then, as it was my last day, I invited Sue and Olson to join Rhoda and me for lunch. When we broke up, Rhoda said she wanted to go into Palm Beach to do some shopping. As she now had her own transport, I gladly opted to return to the apartment.

Sitting on the balcony, I thought over what Dyer had told me and recalled what Val had also told me. Had Vidal really hypnotic powers? If he had, was Val under his influence? If she was, could he get from her that we were lovers?

Remembering her terror and her warning of his viciousness (*he would have us killed!*), I became so uneasy I just couldn't continue to sit on the balcony any longer. I had to find something to do to rid myself of this pressure of growing alarm.

I changed into slacks and an open neck shirt and drove to the golf club. I found Joe Harkness of the American Express hopefully looking for a partner. He brightened when he saw me.

'You're in for a beating, buddy,' he said. 'I'm feeling right on form.'

With Val very much in my thoughts, I was in no mood to concentrate, and I played my worst ever round of golf.

As we went together to the bar, Harkness said, 'Boy! You've certainly things on your mind. Is Dyer worrying you?'

Knowing he would find out sooner or later, I told him, starting from tomorrow, I was going to work for Vidal. The news seemed to shock him out of his jocular mood.

'Is that such a bright idea, Clay?' he asked. 'Of course it's no business of mine, but the last man I would care to work for would be Vidal.'

'He'll probably be tricky, but the money is good and I need a change.'

'But for how long? I have an idea he isn't going to last. This empire he's built gives off a smell. Frankly, I've never slept better since we lost the account. I have a feeling that before long there's going to be a godawful crash.'

I looked sharply at him.

'Just a feeling? Anything to support it?'

'Nothing tangible but people are talking and there's no smoke without fire.' He glanced around to make sure we couldn't be overheard, then went on, 'I know for a fact that when his contract with U-Drive comes up for renewal at the end of this month, they are only going to give him a month's credit instead of six. Once that leaks, all his other creditors will do the same. Has it occurred to you, Clay, that if your people still had his account and learned no one was going to give him six months' credit any longer, wouldn't they follow suit? If Vidal suspected that his credit was going to be cut, it would be a smart move to hire an experienced operator like yourself to handle his travel. At least, he would be saving agency commissions.'

I stared at him. This certainly hadn't occurred to me but I didn't go along with the idea. It had been Val who had made the suggestion. However, I could see that if Vidal did suspect he was only going to get a month's credit from the A.T.S. in the future, he would jump at the idea of employing me.

'Well, it's no skin off my nose,' I said and finished my beer. 'Even if Vidal comes unstuck, I'm safe. Massingham is holding my job open. Let's hope Vidal keeps going long enough for me to pick up some extra money before he goes crash – always providing he is going to crash.'

'I hope so.' He still looked worried. 'I'd better be moving or the little lady will have my hide. See you next week, huh?'

When he had gone, I thought over what he had said. I recalled that after checking with the Credit rating people, Massingham had discovered that Vidal didn't own a thing: that the house, cars, yacht and even Val's jewellery were hired. I remembered my reaction. *A pretty convenient arrangement if you want to skip suddenly.*

If Massingham hadn't assured me my job would be waiting, I would have been worried. As it was, I shrugged. I was in the position of having my cake and eating it.

Leaving the club house, I drove down town and bought groceries for the week-end. The Public Library was across the way from the self-service store and on impulse I dumped the two sacks of groceries in the trunk of the car and entered the library.

A large, matronly looking woman with white hair and twinkling grey eyes, smiled a welcome.

'It's Mr Burden,' she said. 'I was wondering when you would visit us.'

I was nonplussed.

'How do you know my name?' I asked.

She laughed.

'It's part of my job to know all the new arrivals. You're with A.T.S. at the Spanish Bay hotel.'

'Guilty.'

'And what can I do for you, Mr Burden?'

I asked her if she had anything on hypnotism.

'Nothing specialised. There will be a reference in one of our encyclopaedias. I'll get you the volume.'

The information I got from the encyclopaedia did interest

73

me, although it was scanty. I learned that women were more susceptible to hypnotism than men, that mediums (persons hypnotised) could not be ordered to do any act disagreeable to them. They could not be ordered to hurt themselves, to eat food repugnant to them, but they would eat, for example, beef and believe it was lobster if told so by the hypnotist. They would obey any normal order and if told to do so, would not remember what they had done. And finally, hypnotism practised by an unqualified person could be dangerous.

If correct, it was reassuring to know that a medium could not be forced under hypnotism to do something that he/she would not do when in a normal state. If I could rely on that statement then it would seem unlikely that Vidal could obtain a confession from Val that we were lovers.

Still thinking about this and feeling more confident, I drove back to my apartment. I was preparing a chicken salad when Rhoda came in.

'Supper's just ready,' I said. 'Did you get all you wanted?'

'No. Get me a big martini, honey. My feet are killing me.'

I never knew when Rhoda's feet were not killing her.

'What were you looking for then?'

'Nothing particular. I was just looking. Palm Beach is even more expensive than here. That didn't stop Mrs Slinky throwing her husband's money around.'

I stiffened.

'Look, Rhoda, must you always refer to Mrs Vidal as Slinky?'

'Why shouldn't I? Do you object?'

'No.' I fixed the drinks. 'Call her what you like if it amuses you.'

'Thanks, I will. She was in Elizabeth Arden buying the whole shop. She gave me one of those catty-smiles, but she was far too snooty even to say hello.'

'How depressing for you.'

Her eyes snapped.

'Don't be sarcastic! Does she know I am your wife?'

I moved out on to the balcony and began to set the table for dinner.

'Why should she?'

'I wondered if you had told her. After all, she is a customer of mine. Did you tell her?'

'No. Are you ready to eat?'

'Maybe if she had known I was your wife she would have stopped to talk.'

'If you are so anxious to have her talk to you, if I see her, I'll tell her you are my wife.'

'*If* you see her? Of course you'll see her. What do you mean?'

'I think I told you, she is away a great deal.'

She gave me a sly little grin.

'How very depressing for you,' she said and laughed.

* * *

The telephone bell was shrilling in the living room: it brought me awake.

It seemed only a few minutes since I had fallen asleep. We had sat up for the late TV show and had finally got to bed at half past midnight. I was in my first heavy sleep when awakened.

Slightly dazed and cursing, I snapped on the bedside lamp as Rhoda sat up. Her face was smothered in grease and her hair in curlers. She looked like hell.

'What is it?' she mumbled. 'Put the light out!'

'It's the telephone.'

I was groping around for my slippers.

'To hell with it! It's a wrong number. Let it ring!'

Maybe over the years with A.T.S. I had become a slave to the telephone. One thing I could never do was ignore its bell. I went into the living room and snatched up the receiver.

'Burden? That you?'

Startled, I recognised Vidal's high squeaky voice.

'Yes. Is that Mr Vidal?'

'Of course it is, Burden. I have to be in San Salvador at 09.30 tomorrow morning . . . this morning. Arrange it and call me back,' and he hung up.

For a long moment I stared at the telephone receiver

clenched in my hand, then I slowly replaced it on its cradle. I looked at my watch. The time was 03.15.

I had checked the flight schedules to San Salvador when arranging his previous visit and I remembered there was no flight to get him there by 09.30.

My immediate reaction was to call the A.T.S. night service and turn the job over to them. Then I remembered this was Monday morning, and from now on, I was employed by Vidal. This was a job I had to handle myself.

Before leaving my office at the Spanish Bay hotel, I had taken all my reference books and time tables with me. These were my bibles: without them I would be as helpless as any tourist wanting information.

Vidal had said he wanted to be in San Salvador at 09.30. I had an instinctive feeling against calling him back to tell him there were no flights and would he pay for an air taxi? With his millions, an air taxi fare should be chick feed to him.

I called the Florida Air Taxi service and talked to the night manager, Roger Everet.

'Sure, no problem, Mr Burden,' he told me. 'Take off 06.45. Your party can pick up the ticket at the airfield. Okay?'

'Fine. If there is any hitch, I'll call you back. What's the cost?'

'Return?'

'Maybe not. Quote me single and return.'

'Nine hundred and eighty-five. Return thirteen hundred.'

'Make it single unless you hear from me within half an hour.'

'Okay. May I have the name of your party?'

'Mr Henry Vidal, Paradise Largo.'

'What was that again?' His voice sharpened.

I repeated what I had said.

'This is a cash transaction, Mr Burden? We don't give credit.'

'Mr Vidal will expect a month's credit. That's the way he pays.'

'No cash, no ride, Mr Burden. I have instructions.'

76

'It may not be convenient to find cash this early,' I said, beginning to sweat. 'The banks . . .'

'Those are my instructions, Mr Burden. Is it a deal or do you want to cancel?'

'I'll call you back.' I hung up as Rhoda appeared in the doorway.

'What's going on?' she demanded shrilly. 'For God's sake, come to bed! I have to work in a few hours.'

'Go back to bed! Don't bother me!' I snarled and dialled Vidal's number.

'This is Mr Vidal's residence,' a pompous voice said.

'Connect me with Mr Vidal. This is Mr Burden.'

There was a delay, then Vidal came on the line.

'Have you fixed it, Burden?' He sounded irritable.

'There's no flight to get you to San Salvador at 09.30, Mr Vidal. I've reserved an air taxi for you. Take-off time 06.45. Please be at the airfield at 06.15. The ticket will be waiting. Do you want the aircraft to wait at San Salvador? If not I'll book you Pan-Am if you'll let me know when you will be returning.'

'I'll do that myself when I reach San Salvador. I don't want the taxi to wait.'

'Right. There's one little thing, Mr Vidal. The fare is nine hundred and eighty-five, cash,' I leaned heavily on the last word.

'Tell them to put it on my account,' and he hung up.

Cursing under my breath, I dialled his number again. He must have been near the telephone for he answered himself.

'What is it now?' he demanded.

'Burden here again, Mr Vidal. You have no account with Florida Air Taxi service. They want cash.'

'They want . . . WHAT?'

His bellow made me snatch the receiver from my ear.

'The manager was emphatic, Mr Vidal,' I said. 'I'm sorry but the ticket has to be paid for before take-off.'

'No one can treat me like that!' He sounded as if he were going to break a blood vessel. 'Now listen to me, Burden. I'm employing you because my wife tells me you are efficient. Then be efficient! Tell this sonofabitch I expect a month's credit or I'll see he loses his job!' and he slammed down the receiver.

I sat for some moments breathing heavily, then bracing myself, I called the Air Taxi service.

Everet came on the line.

'This is Burden,' I said, my voice trying to drip honey. 'Mr Vidal hasn't that much cash until the banks open. Can't you stretch this as a favour? He could put a lot of business your way if you play nice.'

'No cash, no ride. Those are my instructions, Mr Burden. Sorry.'

'Mr Vidal could get tricky, Mr Everet. He could take this up with your management.'

Everet gave a snorting grunt.

'Did that phony dwarf threaten to get me the gate, Mr Burden?'

'Well, yes. That seemed to be his thinking.'

'Is that right? Would you please give him a personal message from me? Tell him, with my compliments, to go screw himself. Should I repeat that, Mr Burden?'

'No, thank you, Mr Everet. You've made it beautifully clear. No cash, no ride.'

'That's it. Do I cancel?'

'I'll call you back,' I said wearily.

I dialled Vidal's number and waited. As if expecting me, Vidal came on the line.

'Well? Have you fixed it, Burden?' he barked.

'I'm sorry, Mr Vidal. Perhaps I had better repeat exactly what Everet said. No cash, no ride, and with his compliments, please tell him to go screw himself.'

Well, there goes my job, I thought. Having had a tiny taste of it, I wasn't sorry. I would have to find some other way of meeting Val. This way was too much.

'Was that what he said?' Vidal's voice had suddenly gone quiet.

'His exact words.'

'Go screw myself?'

'That is correct.'

To my startled surprise, Vidal gave his short, barking laugh.

'You have more guts than I thought, Burden. Always tell me the truth. You are way ahead of these lousy yes-men I have around me. Tell Everet he'll get cash and I'll be at the airfield at 06.15,' and he hung up.

Five

I ARRIVED at the Vidal residence at 08.50. I had had scarcely
any sleep and I was feeling tense at the thought of seeing Val
again. As soon as I had parked my car, I went to Dyer's office.
As a member of the staff, I didn't bother to announce myself
to the receptioness. I tapped on Dyer's door and entered.

He was sipping a cup of coffee, a big pile of unopened mail
before him.

'Hello,' he said. 'I heard about last night. Never be surprised at the surprises Tiny will surprise you with. As I told
you no hours are sacred to him. Burning to make a start?'

'Where do I go?'

'I'll show you.' He finished his coffee, got to his feet and
moved out of his office. 'You will be working in the residence.
Mrs V. wouldn't want to work here. I've spent the whole
week fixing your office. Consider yourself favoured.' While he
was talking, he led the way along the azalea lined path to the
house. 'Everything fancy, of course. Mrs V. has luxury tastes.'
We entered the house and he led me through a big hall
crammed with armour and old weapons and up a wide staircase, along a passage to a door at the far end. Opening it, he
stood aside and waved me in. 'Make yourself at home. The
big desk is yours. The desk with the I.B.M. is for Mrs V. The
schedules are on your desk. Go to it, brave heart. I must
return to my slum. See you,' and he withdrew.

I leaned against the door and looked around the big, sunlit
room. It was luxurious all right. The big french windows
looked on to the swimming pool. My desk was big enough to
play billiards on. There were four telephones, an inter-com

and nearby a Telex machine. A Grundig recorder stood on a small table by the desk. I went around and sat in the executive chair. Opposite me was a slightly smaller desk, equipped with an I.B.M. Executive, two telephones, a Grundig recorder and an array of pencils and ball points. The room was air conditioned. It was certainly the most luxe office I had yet worked in.

On the snow white blotter were a dozen or so thick envelopes. The time now was 09.00. I wondered when Val would appear. Remembering that Dyer had said I would be busy, I picked up one of the envelopes and opened it.

It contained a brief to transport Mr and Mrs William Jackson for a two week stay in Rangoon, hotel to be arranged, V.I.P. Two passports were included. Visas would be required.

It suddenly dawned on me what I had taken on. If this travel brief had come to me at the A.T.S. office, I would have sent it to Massingham who had the staff to deal quickly and efficiently with it and obtain the visas. Apart from Val who hadn't yet appeared, I had no staff. The Burmese Consulate was in Miami: a trip of over an hour there and back. There was always a delay at any Consulate. I couldn't hope to get the visas back here under four hours: a waste of the whole morning. This just wasn't realistic.

I looked at the intercom, found Dyer's name under one of the switches and called him.

'This is Burden,' I said. 'I want a leg-man to go to Miami right away. Will you fix it?'

'Not my pigeon I am glad to say, old boy. Try Lucas. He handles staff problems. So sorry,' and he snapped up his switch.

I located Bernard Lucas's number, called him and explained my problem.

'We have no one to spare.' His dry voice sounded completely unco-operative. 'I don't know anything about this. I was under the impression we deal with the A.T.S. Why not ask them?'

'We are not dealing with them any more.' I tried to keep the exasperation out of my voice. 'I'm handling the travel end now for Mr Vidal. I want a leg-man.'

'Then you'll have to speak to Mr Vidal. I have no

6

authority to engage additional staff,' and he hung up.

This was something Val would have to cope with, I told myself. I looked at the brief again and saw the Jacksons were due off early the day after tomorrow. This would be cutting it very fine to get their visas in time. At least I could book the flight, lay on a car and fix their hotel accommodation. This I did, using the telephone and the telex. That was as far as I could go with this brief. I put the papers back into the envelope and opened another. This was for transport for Mr Jason, Mr Hamilton, Mr Fremlin and Mr McFeddy to Tokyo. The usual Vidal V.I.P. treatment. Mr Jason needed to be reminded to have a smallpox shot and Mr McFeddy needed a visa. I cursed them both. They were due off in three days' time. I got on to the Jap airlines and booked their flight then telexed the Pacific hotel, Tokyo for accommodation.

But why go on? Each envelope I opened contained some headache or another. Dyer had certainly passed me the buck. There was still no sign of Val. I worked fast but without someone to do the typing I was ham-strung.

Where the hell was Val? The feeling that the work was fast getting on top of me made me angry and uneasy. I looked at my watch. The time was 11.10. Pulling a scratch pad toward me, I methodically wrote down the details of all the flights and the necessary hotel bookings in order of priority. I found out of fourteen briefs, five were immediate and the rest could be left until tomorrow.

Hoping that at any moment Val would appear, I concentrated on the five briefs. I didn't realise it was 13.00 until the intercom buzzed and Dyer's drawling voice said, 'I forgot to mention it, old boy. There's a canteen at the back of my office block. The food's reasonable and cheap.'

'Could I have a sandwich sent up?'

'Ah, yes, I was forgetting you're a desk-lunch man.' The sneer was unmistakable. 'Dial 23 on the green phone. They'll send you what you want.'

'You haven't seen Mrs Vidal?'

'She popped off to Palm Beach. Didn't she look in?'

I drew in a long, slow breath.

'No, she didn't.'

82

'She seemed a little moody. Maybe she forgot it's your first day. Did you get your leg-man?'

'No.'

'Too bad. How are you managing? Quite a lot for you to handle on your own I should imagine.'

'It's under control,' I snapped and switched off.

Popped off to Palm Beach.

It was hard to believe. We hadn't seen each other for over a week. Surely she couldn't have forgotten? Surely she had been counting the days and the hours as I had been. I pushed back my chair and went over to the window. I had to get those visas for Rangoon before 17.00. I looked at the papers covering my desk. I couldn't afford the time to go myself. Then I thought of Sue who always rose to an emergency. I hesitated. If Massingham heard about it, Sue could get into trouble. There was no harm in asking, I told myself. Olson would be out at lunch. Sue would be on her own.

I called her.

'Hello, Clay! I was wondering about you. How are you getting on?'

'I am in a jam, Sue. I've got no staff and I want two visas for Rangoon by 17.00. You'll save my life if you can help me.'

'Have you the passports?'

'Yes.'

'Jake has to go to Miami for visas. I'll tell him to come to you first. He'll be with you in half an hour.'

'You wonderful girl!'

'Clay . . . you better give Jake something. If it got out . . . '

'I'll take care of him. You're a real life saver.'

'Bye now,' and she hung up.

I returned to my chair and sat down, looking at the litter of papers before me. I decided I would have to do my own typing. I was gathering the schedules together when the door jerked open and Val came in.

The sight of her set my heart thumping. She looked marvellous and so chic. She carried a large plastic bag which she tossed on her desk. Then she shut the door.

'Darling Clay! Did you wonder where I had got to?'

I got slowly to my feet.

'Dyer told me.' My voice was husky.

'I just had to go. They're selling off. I've got the most marvellous dress for practically nothing! I must show it to you.'

I reached her, put my arms around her, but she pushed me away.

'No, Clay. Not here!' She was speaking in a whisper. 'It's too dangerous. Anyone could walk in.'

I controlled myself and moved away from her, a feeling of sick disappointment and resentment sweeping over me.

'Never mind the dress, Val,' I said sharply. 'Have you seen what Dyer has left us to handle?'

She frowned.

'What do you mean?'

'There's a hell of a lot of work here and it is urgent. I've been waiting for you.' I picked up the schedules and dropped them on her desk. 'These need your immediate attention. Would you let me have four carbon copies? While you're doing that, I'll fix the flights.'

'But Clay!' She was staring at me, her beautiful eyes shocked. 'You sound worried. What's so important?'

I kept control of my temper.

'Unless you start working, Val, and fast, six V.I.P.s won't take off and we will have fallen down on our first assignment. Judge for yourself how important it is.'

'Clay . . . you're shouting at me!'

'I'm sorry. I've had quite a morning. I've even had to get my ex-secretary to help out. Come on, Val. Let's get stuck into it.'

'But I can't work in this. I must change. This dress looks marvellous but it is a beast to sit in, and besides, darling, I haven't had lunch, have you?'

I moved around her, sat at her desk and pulled the type-writer towards me.

'No. I don't want anything right now. I'll start these while you change. Be as quick as you can, won't you?'

She touched my shoulder lightly.

'I believe you are angry with me.'

'Just be as quick as you can.' Threading paper into the machine, I began to type.

She looked at me for a long moment, then picking up the plastic bag, she left the room.

The buzzer sounded on my desk. Cursing, I crossed over and snapped down the switch.

'Mr Burden? This is the security guard. A messenger on a motorcycle, Jake Lamb, asking for you.'

I said to send him up, then returned to my typing.

Some five minutes later a girl brought Jake in. He stared around the luxurious office, his eyes popping.

'Doing yourself pretty well, aren't you, Mr Burden?' he said.

'Not so bad.' I gave him the passports. 'Get these back with the visas as quick as you can, Jake. It's an emergency.'

'Sure. Miss Harkness told me,' and he winked at me.

As I led him to the door where the girl was waiting I pressed a ten dollar bill into his hand.

When he had gone, I completed one of the schedules and was starting on another when Val came in. She was wearing a white blouse and a dark skirt, and looked wonderful.

'I've ordered sandwiches and martinis,' she said. 'Now I'll take over.'

'Fine. I'll fix the flights.'

I moved out of her chair.

'Not cross with me any longer, darling?'

'No, of course not.'

She sat down. 'I've often thought of this moment, Clay, when we would work together again. Do you like your office?'

I sat down at my desk, aware we were wasting time. As I lifted the receiver, I said, 'Marvellous. If only Dyer hadn't left us with such a pile of urgent work . . .'

There came a tap on the door and a flunkey entered wheeling a trolley on which stood two silver covers, a big cocktail shaker and glasses.

'All right, Ferdy,' Val said. 'We'll help ourselves.'

When he had gone, she got up and poured drinks while I talked to Pan-Am.

'I'm hungry,' she exclaimed. 'Come at eat, Clay,' and she took the covers of neatly cut sandwiches.

'Let's eat while we work,' I said.

'I can't eat and type at the same time. I'll get everything

greasy, and you can't talk on the phone and eat at the same time. Don't be difficult, Clay. Come and eat.'

I gave up. So if these damn V.I.P.s didn't take off, it was just too bad. If Val didn't realise the amount of work we had to do before I went home then that was also too bad.

I joined her at the trolley and took a double martini-gin from her.

'Here's to us, darling,' she said and smiled at me. 'It's fun, isn't it?'

I drank half the cocktail at a gulp and immediately felt better and hungry. We began eating the caviar and smoked salmon sandwiches.

'God! It's been endless . . . this waiting,' she said. 'I thought Monday would never come, didn't you?'

'You can say that again.' I paused, then went on, 'Val, we must have extra help. We need a leg-man to handle the visas and do the odd jobs. I've spoken to Lucas and he says I must speak to Vidal. Can you fix it?'

'Henry won't like it. The man will have to be paid.'

'You can't expect to get him for nothing.' Again I felt a wave of irritation run through me. She was treating this too casually.

'I'll talk to Lucas. He's not co-operative.'

'Look, Val, if you can't fix it, we can't handle this job. It's as simple as that.'

'We won't need visas every day surely?'

'There will be other things for him to do. We must have an outside man.'

'You're not eating, darling.'

I finished my martini.

'I've had enough,' and I returned to my desk.

'Clay . . . '

I paused as I reached for the telephone.

'What is it?'

'Don't get so worked up. We'll manage.'

'If you really want me with you, Val,' I said speaking slowly and deliberately, 'we've not only got to manage, but we've got to have a leg-man!'

I then dialled North-Eastern airlines and asked for Reservations.

'Would you think I was terribly greedy if I had some more sandwiches?' she said. 'They're marvellous, aren't they?' She poured herself another martini. 'Do have some more, darling. You've scarcely eaten anything.'

I was too exasperated to speak. I couldn't even look at her. Then the booking clerk came on the line.

This was a hell of a beginning, I thought as I held on while he checked the flight. Was it going to work? Had she allowed me to kiss her, to hold her in my arms for a brief moment, maybe I wouldn't have been in such a frustrated rage, but that and the fact she was so casual and calm about the mountain of work facing us made me wish to God I was back in the quiet Spanish Bay hotel office with Sue efficiently coping.

Val was still eating a sandwich when I had concluded talking to the clerk. I had Pan-Am, B.O.A.C., and Swiss Air still to call. As I dialled Pan-Am I said, 'For God's sake, Val! Do get started! Look at the time! It's after three!'

Her eyes widened as she picked up another sandwich.

'What's making you so nervy, Clay? Please don't shout at me like this. I don't like it.'

I eased my collar that was choking me.

'I'm sorry. I didn't mean to shout. We must get on with this work!'

The Pan-Am man came on the line and I gave him names and times.

She finished the sandwich, wiped her fingers on a paper napkin and, carrying her martini, went to her desk. She began to type.

Even as I was making the reservations, I was aware that she was pecking and hunting. In the past, she had been the fastest typist I had ever had, making her typewriter sound like an exploding machine gun. This hesitant tap-tap-tap gave me a feeling of panicky despair. At her rate of typing the schedules would take a week to finish! Even I could type four times as fast and I was no typist. I completed my order with Pan-Am, then looked up B.O.A.C.'s telephone number, still listening to the painfully slow tap-tap-tap. Then suddenly she said, 'Oh, hell!' loudly, stared at what she had typed, ripped out the five sheets of paper, crumpled them and threw them violently into her trash basket.

'Don't keep staring at me! You're making me nervous,' she said furiously. 'I haven't touched a typewriter for six years ... what do you expect?'

'Let's change places,' I said, beginning to get desperate. 'You book the flights and I'll do the typing.'

'I'm damned if I will!' Her eyes flashed. 'You do your job! I'll do mine!'

We were glaring at each other when the door opened silently and a man came in.

To say he startled me was an understatement. He looked like a cheap gangster straight out of an old Bogart movie. He had on a grey suit with thick black stripes, a white slouch hat, a black shirt and a white tie. If that wasn't old hat enough, to add to the picture were his long black sideboards, his blue chin and a phony diamond stick pin. He looked like a thug you see in newspaper cartoons.

But he was no joke. There was a deadly stillness about him that increased my heart-beat. His flat, snake's eyes, his small lipless mouth told me as nothing else could that this man, standing in the doorway, was as lethal and as dangerous as a black mamba.

His little eyes moved over me with a contemptuous indifference that was an insult, then he slightly turned his head on his thick bull-like neck and found Val. He moved to her desk and dropped an envelope before her.

'The Boss says to fix it pronto.'

He had a voice like a fall of gravel.

Turning on his heels, he moved out of the room the way a snake moves, swiftly and in complete silence. The door closed behind him.

I looked at Val. Her face was as white as a fresh fall of snow.

The buzzer of my intercom made me start. I snapped down the switch.

'Burden ...'

It was Dyer.

'I'm sending up a brief, old boy. Terribly sorry. I should have handled it last week. Went clean out of my mind. Mr Wernstein has just arrived at the Spanish Bay hotel. Mr

Vidal promised him some deep sea fishing. Lay on a boat and a crew for him, will you? It's all in the brief.'

I stared helplessly at the intercom. I was still trying to recover from the gangster's visit.

Val suddenly appeared at my desk.

'Dyer!' Her voice was shrill. 'You handle it! Understand? We're too busy to bother with fishing boats! You forgot it . . . you fix it!' and leaning past me, she snapped up the switch.

We looked at each other. Faint colour was back in her cheeks, but her eyes were panicky.

'Who was that?' I said and nodded to the door.

'Guilio Gesetti. One of my husband's hatchet men . . . that's what they're called, aren't they?' Her voice was shaking. 'The man who threw acid I told you about. The man who would kill us both if my husband gave him the nod.'

My mouth turned dry. I began to say something, but the words made no sound. I hadn't really believed her when she had warned me of Vidal's thugs, but I believed her now . . . seeing was believing. I felt a chill crawl up my spine.

She returned to her desk, ripped open the envelope Gesetti had left and read the letter.

She drew in a long, slow breath as she looked at me.

'Henry is going to Libya on the 5th . . . that's the day after tomorrow. He returns on the 9th. We are to arrange everything for him.' She forced a smile that didn't reach her eyes. 'We will have almost a week without him, darling. Think of it . . . a whole week!'

Gesetti had thrown such a scare into me I felt no pleasure at the news.

'I'll fix his flight,' I said and reached for the telephone.

*   *   *

Jake Lamb, the A.T.S. messenger, was shown into my office a few minutes to 17.00. With a wide grin and a wink, he handed me the Rangoon visas.

'There you are, Mr Burden.' I saw his eyes stray to Val and his lips pursed into a soundless whistle. 'All in order.'

'Many thanks, Jake. You're a life saver.'

I had completed Vidal's Libyan schedule and was now

waiting impatiently for Val to finish typing it. So far she had only completed one schedule and was now pecking and hunting at the Libyan schedule.

I had the problem of getting the visas to the Jacksons. They were staying at the Palace hotel which was well out of Jake's way, but I had to ask him. I had no one else to send.

He looked dubiously at his watch.

'I'm late as it is. Mr Olson will raise hell.'

I put the visas in an envelope with the schedule and took a five dollar bill from my wallet. I looked at him and lifted my eyebrows.

He grinned.

'Well, okay, Mr Burden: anything to oblige. I can always say I had a flat.'

When he had gone, I looked across at Val.

'That's personally cost me fifteen dollars. Can you now see why we must have a leg-man?'

'Don't talk! I'm busy,' she snapped, then, 'Oh, hell! You've made me make a mistake!'

'I'm sorry.' I knew I didn't sound sorry, but I was too worried to care.

Going to the telex, I began typing a request for accommodation in New York. One of my telephone bells rang.

'Would you get it, please?' I said without looking around.

I heard her mutter something, then she answered the telephone.

She said impatiently, 'Hello? Yes . . . he's here. Who is it? Oh!' A slight pause, then she went on, 'Will you hold it, please?'

'It's for you,' she said in a whisper. 'Your wife!'

We stared at each other. This was something I hadn't foreseen. My hands turned clammy. Had Rhoda recognised Val's voice?

I picked up the receiver.

'Rhoda?'

'That's me. When you buy the bread rolls and the cream, will you also get me two packs of cigarettes? I'm right out.'

I looked at the litter of papers on my desk and then at the desk clock. The time was 17.35.

'I'm sorry, honey, no can do. I'll be working late. You get

them. I'll be lucky if I get back before half past nine.'

'Half past nine?' Her voice shot up. 'For God's sake! What kind of job is this?'

'It happens to be a busy day.' I tried to keep my voice under control. 'First day . . . you know. Look, honey, I'll have to hang up. My desk is loaded.'

'If you think I'm going to wait until nine-thirty before I eat, you're mistaken!' Her voice turned shrill.

'All right . . . all right! Eat when you like! Don't wait for me!' and I hung up.

Val said, her voice unsteady, 'Did she recognise my voice?'

'I don't know and right now I don't give a damn! Let's get on!'

Soon after 18.00, Val finished the Libyan schedule.

'That's number two, thank God! Now I must fly or I'll be late.'

I stared at her as she hurriedly removed the carbons.

'You going?'

'I have to.'

'But there are three more schedules to do, Val.'

'They must wait,' she said impatiently. 'I have a dinner date with the Wernsteins, damn them! Henry arranged it. I can't get out of it.'

'Okay.' I was too depressed to argue. 'If you have to go, you have to go.'

'Don't be cross, darling. It'll be better tomorrow.'

'I hope to God you're right!'

She came over swiftly, kissed my cheek lightly and was gone.

I ran my fingers through my hair. I should have anticipated this, I told myself. How the hell could we possibly have sex in Vidal's own home? It would have been a lot better, easier and safer if I had stayed with the A.T.S.

I was so frustrated that I banged my clenched fists on my desk. After a few minutes I cooled down and wearily looked at the Vidal schedule that Val had typed. It was crowded with typing errors. I suddenly didn't care any more. If Vidal didn't like his wife's typing, he could tell her so. I put the schedule together with the flight ticket and the hotel voucher in an envelope and addressed it to the Intercontinental hotel San Salvador.

Laboriously, I began to type the remaining schedules. It wasn't until 22.00 that I finally cleared my desk.

By the time I had driven out to Miami airport, given the Vidal schedule to an air hostess, who I knew, to deliver to Vidal when she arrived at the Intercontinental hotel in the afternoon, and then driven back to my apartment the time was 23.18.

I found Rhoda watching TV.

'You're late!' she exclaimed, her eyes not moving from the lighted screen. 'Don't talk now . . . this is exciting.'

I went into the kitchen and looked around. There was no sign of any food.

'Did you get anything?' I called.

'No, I forgot. Don't interrupt!'

I fixed myself a whisky and soda, strong enough to knock over a horse. Then I opened a can of beans and not bothering to heat them, I ate them cold from the can.

I finished as the TV programme finished.

Rhoda came into the kitchen. I could tell by the way she stood, her hands on her hips and her face set that I was heading for trouble.

'So Slinky answers the telephone for you,' she said. 'You must feel flattered.'

I was expecting this. I never underestimated Rhoda's shrewdness.

'Mrs Vidal happened to be in the office,' I said, rinsing my glass. 'I was on the telex so she answered.'

'Mrs Vidal *happened* to be in the office? Who do you think you're conning? You told me that whore was away!'

I held on to my rising temper, but only just. I put the glass down.

'Try not to be more vulgar than you can help, Rhoda. I told you Mrs Vidal is away a great deal. She's not away right now. She came in to see if I approved of the office.'

'Don't you dare call me vulgar!' Rhoda screamed. 'If anyone's vulgar it's your precious Slinky with her money and her jewels! If she's not a whore, she looks like one!'

'Have it your own way. I'm going to bed. I'm tired.'

I made to pass her but she blocked my exit.

'Tired! I bet you are!' she shrilled. 'Working until now! Do you think I'm that wet behind the ears? I bet you've been screwing that whore!'

I shouldn't have drunk so much whisky. I did something that was completely out of character and beyond my control. I slapped her face so hard she went staggering into the living room, overbalanced and sat down hard on the floor.

She sat there, staring up at me, her mouth open, her eyes dazed.

I stepped around her and went into the bedroom. I was shaking and sick with myself. I sat on the bed and put my hands to my face.

After some minutes, she came in and keeping away from me, she began to undress. Every now and then a dry little sob escaped her.

These sounds didn't touch me. I was too absorbed in my own despair. The fact that I now fully realised I couldn't make love to Val in Vidal's house and that I would have to plot and plan to get her somewhere safe where I could, gave me such a feeling of suffocating frustration that Rhoda just didn't exist.

Suddenly she said in a snivelling little voice, 'I shouldn't have said that, Clay. You were right to hit me. I deserved it.'

I suppose I should have taken her in my arms then and told her I was also sorry, but I didn't. Instead I said wearily, 'Let's forget it,' and getting up, I began to undress.

'You did hurt me. Really you did.'

'Do you imagine you didn't hurt me?' Reaching for my pyjamas, I moved to the bathroom. 'Let's forget it.'

Later, when we were lying side by side in the dark, she reached for me, but I pushed her hand away.

'Go to sleep,' I said. 'I'm tired even if you're not.'

A callous thing to have said, but I was still smouldering with frustration and I didn't give a damn if I hurt her or not.

I didn't sleep much that night. I thought with dread of the work to be done tomorrow, of Val's pecking and hunting, of looking at her and not being allowed to touch her.

Rhoda was soon asleep. The soft little snorts she always

made when sleeping got so badly on my nerves I was tempte
to wake her, but I didn't.

At 06.30, I slipped out of bed, careful not to wake her.
took my clothes into the bathroom, shaved, showered an
dressed. She was still sleeping when I tip-toed into the kit
chen. I made myself a cup of coffee. There was no bread fo
toast. I saw a pack of cigarettes on the table. She hadn't for
gotten her cigarettes.

As I was putting the cup and saucer in the sink, sh
appeared, looking doleful and in a mess.

'Why are you up so early?' she asked.

'I'm going to the office. I have a load of work still to do
Will you try to remember to get in some bread and cream
If I'm going to be late, I'll call you.'

'Oh, Clay, I wish you hadn't taken this job. I really do
I'm sure it is a mistake.'

I had a sudden uneasy feeling she was right, but I wa
committed.

'You like your car, don't you? See you tonight,' and I lef
her.

*   *   *

Val didn't come to the office until 10.15. There was a guilt
expression in her eyes as she shut the door.

'I'm sorry to be so late, darling,' she said and quickly sa
down behind her desk. 'I had a hell of a night with those tw
old bores and I overslept.'

I had been working steadily since 07.30. In that time I ha
completed six briefs, typed the schedules, arranged the flights
but I had four visas still to cope with.

'We're back on the visa problem, Val. Will you call Luca
and tell him we must have a leg-man pronto?'

Her eyes widened.

'I can't do that. I have no authority.'

'Okay, then we'll get one without authority.' I called a
Employment agency I had had dealings with, told them
needed a boy to run messages and I wanted him fast. The
said they would send someone over within the hour. The cos

would be sixty dollars a week. They had a student on vacation who would welcome the work.

I then went over to the telex machine and sent a telex to Vidal: *Need your authorisation for messenger at sixty per week. Essential. Burden.*

Val just sat there, listening and watching.

'Well, that fixes that,' I said, returning to my desk. 'If your husband kicks, then I'll pay the boy.'

'He won't like it.'

'Too bad. Tell me, Val, who are all those people travelling at his expense?'

'People who work for him. People he has to bribe. He's too smart to give them money. They get their vacations free.'

'Why does he have to bribe them?'

'To get information. He lives on other people's information.'

'Do you know his credit is being cut from six months to one month everywhere? Is he in trouble?'

She stiffened.

'Trouble?'

'I heard his empire could crash. It's no more than talk, but could it?'

She passed the tip of her tongue over her lips.

'He's worth millions.'

'Other men have been worth millions. That doesn't mean a thing. Has he said anything to you? I'm not being curious, Val. I'm thinking of you. If there is a crash, what will you do?'

'He won't crash. He is far too evil.' She shook her head. 'The devil looks after his own.'

At this moment the intercom buzzed and Dyer told me he was sending up three briefs that were immediate.

She had heard what he had said so I didn't have to repeat it.

'Let's get on.' I began on another brief.

She began her peck and hunt routine. After a girl had brought up the briefs and I had studied them, Val's slow tap-tap-tap stretched my nerves to snapping point.

Finally, I could stand it no longer.

'Val! This can't go on! I must have a fast typist! You can

see that, can't you? You're so out of practice we just can't go
on like this. I don't mean to be unkind . . . ' I broke off as I
saw her face crumple in utter despair and she put her arms
across the typewriter and her head on them. Her body began
to shake with sobs.

Alarmed, I went to her, only just restraining myself from
taking her in my arms.

'Val, forgive me!' My frustration and irritation gave way
to remorse and pity. 'I didn't mean to hurt you. Don't be
upset, darling. Let's talk about it. There must be a solution.
Come on, darling, don't give way.'

She straightened up. The haunted, desperate expression in
her eyes shocked me.

'Can't you understand what is happening?' She pressed
the palms of her hands hard against her eyes. 'Do you really
believe I have forgotten how to type? Can't you see the battle
that is going on before your eyes?'

I stared at her.

'Battle? Forgive me but I just don't know what you are
saying.'

She dropped her hands into her lap with a gesture of
despair.

'I've explained and explained. You just don't understand.'
She leaned forward, staring up at me. 'He is punishing me!
The moment I put my fingers on the keyboard, I feel him
taking over, forcing me to make mistakes, paralysing my
fingers so every time I touch a key, it is a struggle. It was he
who forced me to oversleep this morning so I would be late.
It was he who forced me to go to Palm Beach yesterday to
buy a dress I didn't want. He is destroying the confidence I
once had in my efficiency deliberately, gleefully to punish
me.'

Trilby and Svengali: devils and spirits . . . they were all
back again. Helplessly I stared at her, trying to understand,
willing myself to understand.

'But why, Val? Why should he want to punish you?'

She shuddered, her hands turning into fists.

'I won't let him make love to me. After that first night . . .
never, never again! Oh, Clay! I can't talk about it.' She put

96

er hand over her eyes as she whispered, 'Horrible . . .
orrible.'

The telex began to clatter. I spun around, my nerves
rawling.

She caught her breath in a dry, choking sob.

'That's him now.' The fear in her voice chilled me. 'He
lways knows when he is succeeding in punishing me. It
oesn't matter how far away he is. He knows.'

The machine stopped typing.

'Go and look.'

With my heart hammering I went to the machine and
ipped out the paper. It shook in my hands as I read the
nessage.

*Don't bother me with trivialities. Hire any additional staff
ecessary. If Mrs Vidal needs typing assistance, supply it.*
H.V.

Silently I gave the message to Val. When she had read it,
ve stared at each other.

'You see?' Her voice trembled. 'He knows he has suc-
eeded. Now do you believe me? Do you still think I'm being
ysterical? Do you still believe that I am a free agent and not
ompletely in his power . . . that his will hasn't conquered
nine?'

'There must be some way I can help you, Val.'

'But you still don't believe, do you?'

'Yes, I do. I think he has got you under a hypnotic in-
uence. It can be the only answer, but how can I help you?'

She shook her head wearily.

'There is nothing you can do. There is nothing anyone can
o. I thought I was strong enough to fight him, but I'm not.'
he looked away as she said half to herself, 'As long as my
fe lasts, as long as his life lasts, I shall be his slave.'

Then I remembered what Dyer had told me: that he had
napped his fingers and Val had gone into a trance. Without
hinking of the consequences, I lifted my hand.

'Look at me, Val,' I said, then I snapped my finger and
humb together.

Six

THE HANDS of my desk clock moved to 13.15.

Two hours had gone by since that terrible scene I had had
with Val. I was at my desk, still shaken and still too shocked
to deal with the briefs spread before me.

What had I done? I kept asking myself. What evil in
fluence had I released by snapping my fingers? Although
Dyer had warned me, I never expected to get such an alarm
ing reaction. Val had turned into a zombie. All character
seemed to drain out of her face, leaving it blank as if she were
dead. Her eyes became fixed in the stare of the blind.

Then she leaned forward, peering past me at the opposite
wall. 'I will kill you!' she said in a low, fierce whisper. 'I will
never be free until you are dead! Your death is my only
hope!'

As I watched her, unable to move, she slowly stood up.

'You can stand there laughing at me!' She looked and
spoke as if she were seeing someone opposite her, invisible to
me. 'Go on, laugh, you devil! You have destroyed me! Now
it is my turn to destroy you!'

She came around the desk and rushed blindly across the
room, her hands like claws, her lips drawn off her teeth.
She thudded against the wall, reeled back, threw herself a
the wall again, her hands striking blindly.

'Let me go!' she cried, wrestling as if she had someone in
her grasp who was stronger than she and she was being forced
back. 'I'll kill you! I'll kill you!'

There was something so macabre and horrible in this

cene, I could only stand motionless, feeling the hair on the
ape of my neck bristling.

Then she gave a piercing cry and fell on her knees, her
ands trying to tear invisible fingers from her throat.

The fear contorting her face galvanised me into action. I
ushed to her and caught hold of her arms.

'Val!'

She struck me violently across the eyes, blinding me for a
moment. As I staggered back, she straightened up, threw out
her hands as if to ward off a blow, then she fell. The back of
her head struck one of the claw feet of the desk with a sicken-
ng sound, her eyes rolled back and she went limp.

With my heart hammering, panic rising, I ran to her and
bent over her. Her breasts under the white blouse rose and
ell, but she was unconscious.

Shaking, I blundered over to the intercom and called Dyer.

'Who is it?' he demanded petulently. 'I'm just going to
unch.'

'Burden. Get help up here!' I cried. 'Mrs Vidal has had an
accident. Get a doctor! Hurry!'

'Is she hurt?' His voice became efficient and alert.

'Get someone! She's hurt! Get a doctor!'

'At once!'

As I snapped up the switch, Val moaned and I went to her.
She opened her eyes.

'My head! What happened?'

'You fell,' I said. 'Just stay still. Help's coming.'

She caught hold of my hand. Her grip was so fierce it was
painful.

'He was here, wasn't he? You saw him?' She shivered. 'He
tried to kill me! Clay, please . . . don't leave me! Promise?'

'Of course. Stay quiet. The doctor's coming.'

She gave a little sigh, muttered something I couldn't hear,
then her eyes closed and she seemed to drift off into uncon-
sciousness.

The door opened and a middle-aged woman with white
hair, sharp blue eyes and a hard mouth came in.

She looked at Val, then as I stood aside, she knelt by Val's
side. She seemed very efficient and calm. She lifted Val's
right eye-lid, felt her pulse, then stood up.

'I am Mrs Clements, Mr Vidal's housekeeper,' she said. 'It would be more convenient if you would now leave her with me, Mr Burden.'

'She hit her head on the desk,' I said as I moved to the door. My voice was unsteady and husky. 'Are you sure there's nothing I can do?'

'The doctor's coming. She had better stay as she is until he has seen her.'

Moving slowly, my legs shaky, I went down the corridor, down the stairs and out into the garden.

'Burden . . .'

I turned.

Dyer was coming quickly towards me.

'What happened?'

I couldn't keep it to myself.

'She went into a – trance and she fell. She hit her head on the desk.'

He eyed me.

'You look shaken, old boy. What you need is a drink. Come back to my office. Come on,' and putting his hand on my arm, he led me towards the office block.

I heard a car coming up the drive and I turned my head.

'Doctor Fontane,' Dyer said. 'He'll take care of her.'

We entered his office and he produced two big whiskies. I drank and was grateful.

'Sit down. You look as if you've seen a ghost,' he said.

My eyes searched his face. The sneering, jeering expression was gone. His eyes showed genuine concern.

I sat down, gulped down the rest of the drink and set the glass on his desk.

'Did you set her off?' he asked quietly. He snapped his fingers.

I nodded.

'I wasn't thinking.' I certainly wasn't going to tell him the whole truth.

'Yes . . . the way it happened to me. You'll have to tell Tiny, Burden.'

I flinched at the thought of speaking to Vidal.

'Wouldn't it be better to let the doctor do it? He'll be able to say how bad she is.'

'Yes, but Tiny will want it first hand from you. Have another drink?'

'No thanks.'

'Oh, come on. You look as if you need another.' He made two more drinks. 'And Burden, a tip . . . don't tell him nor anyone else about the finger snapping. It wouldn't go down well with Tiny. I suggest you tell him she came over faint and fell.'

I never imagined I could get to like Dyer, but I now found myself liking him.

'Yes, you're right.'

'It's damned odd, isn't it? What do you make of it? It's as if she's been hypnotised. Do you think she has? You know I've wondered about Tiny. He could have hypnotic powers. Once he stared at me and I'll be damned if I didn't feel as if I was suddenly floating. A most odd sensation. Do you think he hypnotises her?'

I hedged.

'Why should he?'

'I've been thinking about her: the set-up puzzles me. I remember Doctor Rappach, a friend of mine, told me that very often glamorous looking women like Mrs V. are frigid. Rappach knows what he is talking about. He uses hypnotism in his work.'

I stared at him.

'You didn't tell him about Mrs Vidal?'

He looked shocked.

'Good God, no! I may be curious, but I don't gossip. He told me an odd story about a man who had hypnotic powers. His wife was frigid and he used to hypnotise her to release her when they had sex. It was a great success. She didn't even know she had had sex with him, but after a while she became neurotic and Rappach had to talk seriously to the husband. I'm only guessing, of course, but it is possible that Mrs V. isn't all that satisfactory bed-wise and Tiny releases her.'

I turned cold and sick.

Could this be happening to Val?

I won't let him make love to me. Her voice echoed in my mind, and her despairing whisper, *horrible, horrible.*

'You look bad,' Dyer said with concern. 'Why don't you go home? I can see you're really upset.'

I drank some more of the whisky.

'I guess I am. When she hit her head ... I thought she had killed herself.'

'You go home.'

'No, I won't do that. I'll get back to my desk. I still have a lot of work to do.'

'Don't forget to tell the quack to contact Tiny.'

I was lucky to meet Dr Fontane as he came down the stairs. He was like a stork: tall, thin with a hooked nose and small beady eyes.

I introduced myself.

'How is she, doctor?'

'She has a nasty cut at the back of her head. Nothing serious. It would be better for her to stay in bed for a few days.'

'Mr Vidal should be informed.'

He smiled sourly.

'I have already spoken to him.' Nodding, he went down the steps to his car.

I returned to my office and closed the door. My mind was seething. As I sat down at my desk, the telephone bell rang.

I had an instinctive feeling it was Vidal calling and I hesitated, then, my heart beating violently, I lifted the receiver.

'Burden?' His squeaky voice jarred my nerves.

'Yes, Mr Vidal.'

'What happened? That fool of a doctor said Mrs Vidal fainted and hit her head. I've never known her to faint. You were there. What happened?'

I licked my dry lips.

'I don't know, Mr Vidal. I was on the telex. My back was turned. I heard Mrs Vidal get up, then the sound of her fall.'

'Do you think she fainted?'

'I think she must have.'

There was a pause, then he gave his short, barking laugh.

'Women!' Again a pause, then he asked, 'How is she getting on with the work?'

'All right, Mr Vidal.'

'Burden! Remember what I said! Always tell me the

truth!' The snap in his voice made me stiffen. 'I will repeat the question: how is my wife getting on with the work?'

I was about to repeat my answer when I remembered that within an hour or so he would get the schedule, crammed with typing errors. He would know who had typed it. I couldn't afford to be caught in a lie if I was to remain close to Val.

'Well, of course, she is a little out of practice,' I said. 'That's to be expected after a six year lay-off.'

'Is she being efficient?'

'She doesn't have to be efficient. That is my prerogative, Mr Vidal.'

He laughed.

'A tactful man. The doctor tells me she should stay in bed for a few days. Get yourself a secretary, Burden. My wife will soon get tired of office routine. I know women. They like to talk about work, but when it comes to the crunch they start throwing faints.'

I was now hating him so violently that if he had been in the office I would have struck him.

'I'll do that, Mr Vidal,' I said.

'I want an efficient service, Burden. See to it,' and he hung up.

As I replaced the receiver, I looked at the briefs still to be done. There was no time now to think about what had happened, what Dyer had said. I had to get these briefs cleared.

I called the Employment agency and asked them to send me a top class secretary on a temporary basis.

'This is an emergency,' I said. 'Put her in a taxi and get her to me as quickly as you can.'

When I mentioned Henry Vidal's name, the woman in charge said a girl would be with me in half an hour.

'I'll send you Connie Hagen. She is exceptionally good. Will you need her long?'

'A week, maybe two weeks. I'm not sure.'

'All right, Mr Burden. She'll be along.' She then asked, 'Did that boy show up ... the messenger you wanted?'

I had forgotten about him.

'Not yet.'

'He'll be along any moment. I told him to have his lunch first.'

Within ten minutes, the boy arrived. His name was Ray Potter, a gangling, long haired, amiable type who seemed painfully anxious to please.

I explained about how to obtain visas, gave him the passports and the addresses of the various consulates and sent him on his way.

I then got down to the briefs. What with telexing and telephoning and checking my reference books, I had no time to think of Val.

Connie Hagen arrived. She was around eighteen or twenty years of age, and the fattest girl I have yet seen which is saying something in this county of grossly fat women. Her round face revealed efficiency, humour and kindness. I liked her on sight. As with most fat girls, she wore skin tight trousers and a blouse that scarcely held under the pressure of her enormous breasts.

I gave her three schedules to type. The moment her fat little fingers dropped on to the keyboard, I knew I had found the support I needed.

The three schedules were finished in a quarter of an hour. A quick look at them showed perfect typing. I then gave her a list of flights to book and left her to it.

We worked at top pressure until 17.45. Potter returned with the visas. I gave him four of the schedules to deliver to various hotels, assuring him he wouldn't have to work this hard tomorrow.

'I don't mind work, Mr Burden,' he said, grinning. 'I just want to earn what I'm being paid.'

When he had gone, Connie opened her handbag and took from it a paper sack.

'Like a bite, Mr Burden?' she asked. 'I always like a little bite before supper. Liver sausage on rye.'

'No, thanks. We're nearly through.' I looked with unbelieving eyes at my now empty desk top.

She took a big bite out of the sandwich, munched and nodded her satisfaction.

'I can't get over me working for Mr Vidal,' she exclaimed. 'Gosh! And in this marvellous house! Won't I bend my boy friend's ears tonight! I'll have you know, Mr Burden, it is a real privilege to work for Mr Vidal.'

This remark turned my mood sour. Up to now, I had been so occupied both Val and Vidal had gone out of my mind.

'Well, let's finish,' I said curtly. 'It's getting on for six.'

At 18.10, I had cleared the last schedule. Connie, still eating, put the cover on the I.B.M.

'What time tomorrow, Mr Burden?'

'Nine o'clock, please.'

'I'll be here. Nightie-night,' and away she went, swinging her massive hips, as light as a thistle-down on her fat little feet, apparently without a care in the world.

*　　*　　*

There was no rush for me to get home. I had warned Rhoda that I might be late. I had much thinking to do and concentration would be impossible with her fussing around.

I sat at my desk. I first thought of what Dyer had said. Was it possible that Vidal was taking advantage of Val under hypnotism and was having intercourse with her without her knowledge? The thought turned me hot with frustrated rage. Could any man be so despicable? I remembered what she had told me: *He is evil! He is a devil!* If he was doing this evil thing, how could I protect her? Should I warn her? After more thought, I decided it would be cruel to do so without having a solution to offer. Had she not said she was no longer a free agent and was completely in his power and that his will had conquered hers? Now that I had more insight of what could be happening, it seemed to me she wouldn't have made such an admission unless it was true.

There is nothing you can do, she had said. *There is nothing anyone can do.*

I refused to accept such a defeatist attitude. I was determined somehow to help her, but I did realise how dangerous it was for me to meddle with this power Vidal appeared to have. In my ignorance I could do harm as I had done in this irresponsible finger snapping episode.

First, then I told myself, I must find out more about hypnotism. I must consult an expert, but who? I thought of

105

Dyer's friend, Dr Rappach. I hesitated. Doctors were not supposed to talk about their patients, yet this doctor had told Dyer about the man who had hypnotised his wife. I wouldn't want it to get back to Dyer that I had been making inquiries. I felt sure the doctor hadn't mentioned names. If I approached him tactfully it should be safe enough. I reached for the telephone book. There he was: *Dr Hugo Rappach, neurologist. 1141, West Street, West Palm Beach.*

Not the best district to live in. West Palm Beach was the suburb of Palm Beach where the workers lived and where there was a large Harlem quarter.

I dialled his number.

'This is Doctor Rappach.' A thick, deep voice that gave me an impression of age.

'My name is George Fellows, doctor,' I said. The phony name belonged to one of the V.I.P.s for whom I had provided tickets. 'I would like to consult you on the subject of hypnotism. Could you give me an appointment, please?'

There was a pause.

'Have you been recommended to me, Mr Fellows?'

'Your name cropped up at a party I was attending. Someone said you used hypnotism sometimes on your patients.'

'Was it someone I know?' The voice was polite but perhaps now a little cautious.

'I forget his name, doctor: short, thickset, balding. You know how it is at a party.' I forced a little laugh. 'Names come, names go.'

'And you are interested in hypnotism. May I ask why?'

I trotted out the hairy excuse so often used.

'I'm writing a novel, doctor, and I want my facts right. Naturally, I would pay your usual consulting fee.'

'I am very busy, Mr Fellows . . . ' A pause. We both breathed at each other over the line. 'However, I could find time to see you if nine o'clock would be convenient.'

'21.00, tonight?'

'Yes.'

'That's fine, doctor. I'll be along.'

We both hung up.

I went back to my thinking.

Twice during our talks together, Val had mentioned Trilby

and Svengali. She had said: *I was a Trilby to his Svengali.*

Who was Trilby? Who was Svengali? Wasn't there once a classical novel called *Trilby*? I had vaguely heard of it, but had never read it. Could this book give me a clue?

It was possible the Public Library would have a copy. I had to pass the Library on my way home. It shut at 20.00. I had plenty of time. I decided to get the book right away.

Then Mrs Clements came in.

'Ah, Mr Burden, there you are. I was afraid you had gone. Mrs Vidal is asking for you.' Her hard blue eyes registered disapproval. 'She is worrying about Mr Vidal's trip to Libya. She won't sleep until you assure her there are no hitches.'

My heart gave a little bound. Val knew the schedule was tied up. This was her excuse to Mrs Clements to see me.

I opened a drawer and took from it one of the schedules waiting completion of a visa.

'There is one small point that Mrs Vidal was attending to herself. I would be glad of the opportunity to get it settled.'

'If you will come with me.'

As we walked along the corridor, she said, 'Please don't stay long. She should be resting.'

'It'll take a very few minutes.'

She paused at the door at the far end of the passage, tapped, opened the door and stood aside for me to enter.

'Mr Burden,' she said and left, closing the door quietly after her.

Val lay in the big double bed. The shades were drawn against the evening sun. The room was cool and luxuriously furnished.

I was shocked to see how white she was: her dark eyes pools of fear and anxiety.

She held out her hand to me. I went to her, longing to take her in my arms. Her hand felt dry and cold.

'How are you, my darling?' I asked, keeping my voice low.

'I'm so glad you have come.' She motioned me to sit on the bed. She kept hold of my hand. 'What happened? I remember being at my desk and then finding myself in bed. What happened?'

So Dyer hadn't lied to me. He had said she remembered nothing when she came out of the trance. Should I tell her?

107

Looking at her, fearful, white and feeling her trembling, I decided not to.

'I don't know, Val. I wasn't looking at you. I heard you fall. You must have fainted.'

'No! I've never fainted in my life!' Her grip on my hand tightened. 'It has happened to me before. I have been reading in the living room, then suddenly I find myself in bed.' She shivered. 'I checked the time. There was a blank space of over an hour! It has happened eight times!' She looked at me. The fear in her eyes chilled me. 'He is responsible! I know he is!'

I was now convinced that he was. I now believed everything she had told me. This wasn't hysteria. I was sure she was under the influence of this man.

'I'm going to do everything I can to help you,' I said. 'You're no longer alone, Val. You have me.'

She pressed her hands to her head in a gesture of despair.

'There is nothing you can do. He has won the battle!'

'There is something I can do and I'm going to do it!'

She looked up at me, her expression made my heart contract.

'Forget me, Clay. How are you getting on? Have you replaced me already?'

'I have a girl who is doing the typing. I had to get her! It is the only way I can stay close to you.'

'Is she as efficient as I used to be?' She bit back a sob. 'I'm no longer efficient, no longer good for anything . . . he has destroyed me.'

I heard footsteps. Hurriedly I stood up and moved away from the bed. A tap came on the door and Mrs Clements came in.

'It is time for Mrs Vidal's tranquilliser, Mr Burden.'

'I'm just going.' To Val, I said, 'There is nothing to worry about now, Mrs Vidal. I'll take care of it.'

'Thank you.'

As I walked down the corridor and down the stairs, the picture of her despair tormented me.

'Trust me, trust me,' I kept saying to myself. 'Val, darling, somehow I will help you.'

It took me only ten minutes to reach the Public Library.

The time now was 19.15. The librarian smiled at me as I approached.

'Hello, Mr Burden. Are you still interested in hypnotism?'

'You have a good memory.' I paused in front of her desk.

'It's not bad. Won't you sit down?'

I glanced around the big library as I sat down. There were only a few students at the reading desks.

'Am I right in thinking there is a book called *Trilby* ... an old classic?' I asked.

She nodded.

'There are two books so called. One written in 1833 by Charles Nodler. The other by George du Maurier in 1895. I would imagine it is du Maurier's book that you are interested in. It has to do with mesmerism.'

I stared at her, startled.

'Your memory is fantastic!'

She laughed.

'Not fantastic. I had an inquiry for the book a couple of weeks ago. I looked it up. You are having the benefit of my research.'

'Have you a copy?'

'Gracious no, Mr Burden. We do have some of the English classics such as Dickens and Scott, but not du Maurier who is never asked for these days.'

'And yet you have two inquiries within two weeks?'

'That is true. A coincidence. I doubt if I could get a copy now unless I tried in England.'

I was disappointed.

'Did you read it?' I asked.

'I have read most of the English classics, Mr Burden.'

'I believe a character called Svengali appears in the book?'

'Indeed, yes. He played an important role in the plot. I think it is fair to say that it was because of this character the book became quite a sensation.'

'In what way? Could you give me an idea of the plot?'

'Very briefly, Svengali, a Hungarian musician, meets a young girl, Trilby, who is struggling to make a living. She is represented as being remarkably beautiful with a perfect figure and, if I remember rightly, an angelic disposition. Svengali is a hypnotist. Under his hypnotic influence, he

109

teaches Trilby to sing. She has no voice nor technique, but so powerful is his influence that she becomes, overnight, the finest singer that ever lived. Royalty, Emperors and dukes flock to hear her and Svengali becomes immensely rich. Then, one night, when she was singing in London before a distinguished audience, Svengali, sitting in a stage box, dies of a heart attack. Without his hypnotic influence, Trilby loses her voice and eventually dies of starvation. That is the story, Mr Burden.' She smiled. 'It is melodrama, of course, but enormously popular at the time. I doubt if you would have the patience to read the book itself. It is over long for modern tastes.'

I had listened to what she had told me with intense interest.

'Would it be impertinent to ask who the other inquirer was?'

'I can't tell you. I have never seen her before. She was very elegantly dressed and quite beautiful, dark with large blue eyes. I was a little worried about her. She seemed so tense and anxious.'

Val!

'Well, thank you,' I said and got to my feet. 'I am most grateful.'

As I walked back to my car, I looked at my watch. The time was 19.45. There was no point returning home and then driving to West Palm Beach. I still had some thinking to do. I got in my car and drove to a nearby Howard Johnson restaurant. Finding a corner table away from the noisy tourists, I ordered a club sandwich, then shut myself in a telephone booth. I called Rhoda.

'Honey, I'm going to be late,' I said when she came on the line. 'I won't be back until ten. Don't wait supper.'

'Is this going to happen every night?' Rhoda demanded crossly.

'I hope not. How have things been with you?'

'The usual. Are you still mad at me?'

'I told you to forget it. I've forgotten it.' My mind was miles away from this flat conversation.

'Well, at least I apologised. I think you could apologise too. My face still hurts.'

110

'I apologise.'

A pause, then she said, 'Well, I'll go down and get something to eat. I'm hungry.'

'Yes, do that. See you, honey,' and I hung up.

What a conversation! I thought as I made my way back to my table.

The club sandwich was waiting for me. While I ate, I thought of what I was going to say to Dr Rappach.

* * *

West Street, West Palm Beach was on the fringe of the Harlem quarter. It was a long, narrow street lined on either side by dilapidated clap-board bungalows with tiny weed-choked gardens, protected by rotting wooden fences.

Puerto Ricans, Spaniards and a few black families sat on verandas or on the kerb talking, playing cards, dozing. Some of the women nursed babies.

As I drove down the street, looking for No. 1141, I was aware of curious eyes, hostile eyes and indifferent eyes watching me.

I found the bungalow at the far end of the street. For a long moment I remained in the car, staring at the wooden plaque on which the number was painted, unable to believe that this was the residence of Dr Hugo Rappach, neurologist. The building was secured by rusty cables against hurricanes. There was a water tank on a brick foundation with a leaky pipe leading into the bungalow. The clap-board had once been white but was now a dirty grey. The path, through a tangle of weeds, that led to the front door was littered with scraps of paper and fruit peel, blown in from the street. Dirty net curtains screened the dusty windows. One wooden shutter sagged on a broken hinge.

Could this possibly be the home of Dr Rappach?

Leaving the car, I eased open the wooden gate, walked up the path, up three steps and on to the stoop that creaked under my weight. The front door had long lost its paint. Three deep slits in the wood would let in the wind and the rain. There was no bell, no knocker, so I rapped with my knuckles. As I stood in the humid heat, I was aware that I

was being stared at. I glanced over my shoulder. The bun
galows opposite all had verandas on which sat an assortmen
of young, elderly and old black people. They were like statue
carved out of ebony, motionless with curiosity.

The door opened and a man stood before me: tall, lear
with a mane of white hair, coarse Negro features, a whit
pitted leathery skin. He was old. At a guess eighty-five or -six
He held himself very upright as if to challenge his age. A
I looked at him, I became aware of the compelling power i
his piercing black eyes.

'Mr Fellows?' I recognised the thick, deep voice.

'That's right,' I said. 'You are Dr Rappach?'

'Yes. Come in. I see my children out there are wondering
who you are. They have little to live for except to be curious.

He led me into a dusty, untidy room with a desk, a chai
behind the desk, a lot of books, a settee and a wooden kitche
chair facing the desk.

'This, Mr Fellows, is my consulting room,' he said, movin
around the desk. 'Take the settee. I won't ask you to use th
hard chair. That is for my patients.' He sat down behind th
desk and put his old, blue veined hands on the desk to
while he surveyed me.

Feeling slightly bewildered, I sat down on the settee tha
creaked and I had to shift as a broken spring dug into me
Could this old man, half white, half black, living in thi
poverty possibly be a friend of the elegant Vernon Dyer
Could he possibly be a neurologist?

'I see you are puzzled, Mr Fellows. That is understandable
Let me explain,' he said. 'If I didn't live in these condition
my children wouldn't come to me. By coming to me the
imagine they are doing me a favour. As they need my help i
is a satisfactory arrangement. I charge them 25 cents a visit.
He smiled, showing his big yellow teeth. 'I have retired from
active practice. At one time I had my own clinic. Now I an
old, now I have enough money to take care of my modes
needs I live in this pig-sty to take care of the many sick an
troubled people who live around me. It is not entirely selfles
I regard it as my insurance for an after life.'

I relaxed.

'All honour to you, doctor,' I said. 'My congratulations.'

'That is something I don't need.' He looked at the cheap watch on his thin wrist. 'I can give you twenty minutes, Mr Fellows. What can I do for you?'

While at the restaurant I had prepared my story. I was confident he would accept it.

'As I explained over the telephone, I am developing a plot for a novel,' I said. 'The situation is this: a man, call him Dokes, has hypnotic powers. He works in night clubs. A girl, call her Mary, comes with a party to the night club for an evening of fun. Urged on by her friends, she allows herself to be hypnotised. She does the usual silly things a hypnotist entertainer makes his subject do. Dokes is a sensualist. The girl attracts him physically and he is determined to seduce her. I won't bother you with the build-up, Doctor. It is enough to say Dokes finds out where Mary lives, breaks into her apartment and because he has already hypnotised her, he has only to snap his fingers to put her in a trance. While in his trance, he rapes her. On waking the following morning, she has no recollection of what has happened. From then on, when in the mood, Dokes visits and rapes her. That is part of my plot. Before I develop it, I want to know if it is feasible.'

The old black eyes regarded me.

'If I may say so, Mr Fellows, your plot is not entirely original. The situation as you describe it actually happened in the eighteenth century to a French countess who was seduced under hypnotism by a pupil of Cagliostro, a famous hypnotist.'

I felt the blood leave my face.

'So it really could happen?'

'Yes, it could happen.'

This was something I couldn't bear to accept.

'But I understand, Doctor, from what I have read that no one when under hypnotic influence can be made to do anything repugnant to them. If this is correct, then surely no woman can be raped under hypnotic influence?'

'In most cases what you say is correct, Mr Fellows, but not in every case. Much depends on the power of the hypnotist and on his subject. Some subjects have much stronger wills to resist than others. It has been said that Rasputin had the power to seduce. Cagliostro certainly had.'

113

I was now feeling so bad, I wanted to terminate this interview as quickly as I could.

'One other question. If she left the town would it be possible for Dokes to retain his influence over her? Does distance matter?'

'That would depend on his power. If it was considerable, then she could even leave the country and he could still keep hypnotic contact with her.'

'Is that a scientific fact?'

He moved impatiently.

'All the facts I am giving you, Mr Fellows, are scientific facts. I have a number of patients who have moved from this district and now live quite some distance away. I still keep in contact with them. They will write or telephone and I can ease their troubles by my hypnotic influence.'

Everything he had told me so far confirmed what Val had said. A feeling of despair was laying hold on me.

'How can Mary break away from Dokes's influence? It is important for her to do so to tie up my plot.'

'Realistically, Mr Fellows, that is not possible. You have created a situation and you are stuck with it. Hypnotism in the hands of amateurs is extremely dangerous. Unless Dokes himself releases her or unless he dies, your heroine will remain in his power indefinitely.'

Grasping at straws, I asked, 'Suppose she went to someone like you, Doctor? Couldn't this expert counteract Dokes's influence?'

He shook his head.

'I am afraid not, nor should he attempt to do so. I certainly wouldn't. We have assumed, to make your plot realistic, that Dokes is no ordinary hypnotist. It then follows that a counter-influence from another hypnotist would create such a violent struggle in the subject's mind that she would, without doubt, suffer very serious mental damage.'

I took out my handkerchief and wiped my sweating hands.

'So the only solution would be for someone to persuade Dokes to release her?'

'That or a timely heart attack. There is an old classic *Trilby . . .*'

114

'I know it. Svengali died of a heart attack and Trilby could no longer sing.'

'Exactly, Mr Fellows.'

'I wouldn't want to use the same solution in my book.'

He lifted his old shoulders and again looked at his watch.

'Well, if he couldn't be persuaded to release her, then he would have to die. He could meet with an accident. I am sure you are inventive enough to dispose of Dokes, Mr Fellows, without any suggestions from me.' He smiled. 'If it were a thriller you are writing, she could, of course, murder him, couldn't she?'

Seven

'WELL NOW, Dr Rappach, let us imagine we are continuing our conversation although I have already paid you a fifty dollar fee, shaken your hand and driven away from the curious eyes of your children. I am parked on a lonely stretch of beach with only the palm trees to listen to our conversation.

'First, let me thank you for your valuable time, Dr Rappach. I hope you don't feel that you could have been more usefully employed than listening to the plot of my novel. You told me you charge your patients a quarter. Well, at least, my fifty dollars represents quite a number of patients. I do assure you you gave me value for money.

'You have confirmed what I was reluctant to accept: that there is only one solution to save Val. You said it. Val said it herself.

'She said: *As long as my life lasts, as long as his life lasts, I shall be his slave.*

'You, Doctor, said the same thing only in different words: *Unless Dokes himself releases her or unless he dies, your heroine will remain in his power indefinitely.*

'So I am now convinced that only Vidal's death will release her. It is as simple and as complicated as that. Complicated because to look at him, you couldn't imagine him dying for many years to come. He is a man in his prime, bursting with energy, a non-smoker, a non-drinker: a man who takes care of himself.

'And yet his death is the only solution if Val is to be freed of his influence.

'You said, Doctor, *If it were a thriller you are writing, she could, of course, murder him, couldn't she?*'

The hot wind blew through the open car window and yet I felt cold.

'It is a valuable suggestion, Doctor, but not the right one .. nearly right, but not quite. It is valuable because I hadn't thought of murder to solve this problem. To prove to you that your suggestion that Val should murder him is wrong, I have to tell you that she means more to me than life itself. This sounds dramatic, doesn't it? But it is a fact. I have never ceased to love Val from the moment I met her, six years ago. Murder means risk. I would never allow Val to be exposed to any risk if I could help it. But all the same your suggestion is valuable. I would accept the risk. Now you ask if I feel capable of murdering Vidal. Before I can answer that question, let us first take a look at Vidal. I don't believe in devils, but if devils do exist as Val says they do – and she has more experience of that kind of thing than I have – then Vidal could be a devil. A man who can rape a woman under the influence of hypnotic power, who will destroy her confidence in herself and who will reduce her to a despairing, frightened cipher such as she had become, must be devilish. You say there are many people like him and it is the business of the police and the courts of law to deal with them. Yes, but you haven't suggested that I should go to the police. You know as well as I do the police would dismiss my story as the ravings of just another nutter, envious of a millionaire tycoon.

'You say I haven't yet answered your question: do I feel capable of murdering Vidal? Frankly, as I sit here in the dark of my car under the palm trees that are swaying and creaking in the rising wind, with the lights of Paradise City distant across the causeway, the thought of killing Vidal doesn't make me flinch. It doesn't make me flinch so long as the thought remains a thought. I am now convinced that Vidal's death is not only the one possible solution, but the right one. By murdering him, Val and I could pick up the threads that he snapped six years ago. We could get married and live happily ever after. I am already married? Yes, but it is no real marriage. Even Rhoda would agree about that. If Rhoda would be willing to divorce me and Vidal dies, then the dream I have lived for over six years would finally come about. You think I would have Vidal's death on my conscience for the rest of my days? I wonder. You could be right, of course, but maybe I could convince myself that the end does justify the means and it would not worry my conscience. You again press the question: am I capable of committing murder? There you have a point. There are some people who have no compunction about taking life. My father was like that. He was a small time farmer and not a day passed without him coming from the fields carrying some dead animal: a rabbit, a hare, a badger or a fox. He was a remarkable shot. No pheasant, pigeon nor wild duck had a chance against his skill. He wanted to teach me to shoot but killing made me sick to my stomach. My father despised me for refusing to kill and I despised him for killing. So coming back to your question as to whether I feel capable of killing Vidal the answer is that I don't know. I can kill him in my mind, I can try to make a plan to kill him so Val and I would never be suspected and if by killing him I could restore her to her old wonderful self of six years ago then I think I could even live with my conscience. But when the time comes, I admit it would be a toss-up whether I could do it. I do know I could never sneak up on him and kill him in cold blood. It would depend on the circumstances. I think I might do it if I were provoked.'

Carried by the wind a warm drop of rain came in through the open car window and splashed on my hand. My mind jerked back to reality. The wind was now roaring through the palm trees and the sea was turbulent. Heavy, black clouds began to blot out the moon. A streak of lightning split the sky followed by a deafening clap of thunder. Down came the rain: a steel curtain of wet violence.

I hurriedly wound up the window, set the windscreen wipers in motion, started the engine and flicked on the air conditioner.

For the moment, the period of thinking was over. There was time. Vidal wouldn't return for another six days.

I headed for home.

*　　*　　*

For the next two days, it rained incessantly.

When Rhoda was at home she was either glued to a maga-zine or to the goggle box. She informed me that the weather service reported that there was a hurricane building up off the West Indies. This was the cause of the spell of bad weather. It was too early yet to say if the hurricane would be heading our way.

My mind was far too occupied to bother about hurricanes.

During those two days I had no news of Val. I was afraid to ask Dyer, still more afraid to seek out Mrs Clements and ask her for news. I was alarmed to see from my office window Dr Fontane arrive and depart twice a day. Surely these twice daily visits must mean that Val was very ill. It tormented me that I dare not ask nor show interest. I would have given any-thing to have gone to her room to find out what was happen-ing, but the risk was too great.

At night, with Rhoda asleep at my side, I thought of Vidal. With the wind and the rain slamming against the window, I thought myself closer and closer to the acceptance of murder.

'Probably you won't have the guts to kill him,' I told my-self, 'but if you manage to screw up enough guts, how do you plan to do it? What kind of a jerk would you be if suddenly you had the opportunity and were without the means?'

Vidal presented a problem. Physically, he was at least three times as powerful as I was. By his movements, I was sure his reflexes were quicker than mine. The only safe and sure way to kill him was to shoot him. But I knew nothing about guns. I had had my chance to learn when I was a kid, but I hadn't taken it. All the same it would have to be done with a gun. If I got close enough to him, I should be able to kill him. So I decided to kill him – if I was going to kill him – with a gun.

But where to get the gun? I would have to be careful. The gun must not be traced to me. The safest place was a pawn shop. From what I had read you could buy a gun from a pawn broker, no questions asked. There must be pawn shops in West Palm Beach. If I could leave my desk for a couple of hours, I would go there and see if I could buy a gun.

I woke to find the sun shining, although the wind was still brisk. While Rhoda and I had breakfast, she talked about the hurricane.

'I'm scared it'll head this way,' she said. 'I was talking to a client yesterday and she said it is really terrible when a hurricane arrives. She remembers the last one, three years ago. The damage was awful and ten people were drowned. Just imagine!'

I finished my coffee.

'It hasn't yet arrived.' I got to my feet. 'I must be moving.'

'It's serious, Clay.' Her eyes were round with worry. She loved to dramatise any situation, and of course, a thing like a hurricane was just her meat. 'We could be marooned! We could even run short of food!'

'Well, see you, honey.' I was only half listening to what she was saying. 'If I'm going to be late back, I'll call you.'

'You're too busy thinking about your stinking work to bother about me!' she exclaimed, suddenly angry. 'You don't give a damn if I'm worried or not!'

'I too have my problems, Rhoda,' I said and picking up my brief case, I left her.

As I was parking my car, Dyer drove up in his E-type Jaguar.

'Hello, old boy,' he said. 'Haven't seen you for a couple of days. Mavis will have sorted the mail by now. Want to see if there's anything for you?'

'Sure. What's this about a hurricane? My wife is getting worked up about it.'

'We haven't had one this way for three years. I guess we're due one.' He led his way into his office. 'There's always a chance it'll blow itself out before it reaches us.'

He sat behind his desk and flicked through the mail, then he handed me three fat envelopes.

'There you are. I hope they aren't headaches.' He grinned. 'How's your new typist?'

'She's excellent. That raises a point. I hired her on a temporary basis. How is Mrs Vidal?' I opened one of the envelopes so I need not look at him. My mouth was dry and my heart was thumping.

'If your typist is good, Burden, my advice to you is to keep her on a permanent basis. It's my bet Mrs V. won't be doing any work for some time, if ever.'

I looked up and stared at him.

'Is she that bad?'

'Confidentially and don't pass this on, she is in one of those odd trances of hers.' He lit a cigarette and pushed the silver box towards me. 'Although he doesn't say so, Fontane is foxed. Of course he doesn't know that she could be hypnotised and I'm not telling him. He would think I was out of my mind. He's bringing a specialist to look at her this morning.'

Huskily, I asked, 'Have you seen her?'

'No, but Mrs Clements is with her most of the time. She tells me Mrs V. is in a semi-coma, won't talk, eats practically nothing . . . in fact, doing her zombie act. She appears, according to Mrs Clements, to have lost all interest in life.'

He has destroyed me!

'Couldn't you get your friend, Dr Rappach, to look at her?'

'Not a chance. That old wreck? He's beyond helping anyone except his nigger children as he calls them.'

'I thought you were a friend of his?'

'I met him at a charity do. He amused me and I gave him money for his deserving nuts. He's not a bad old boy.'

'Shouldn't you tell Dr Fontane about the finger snapping business?'

'That would be sticking my neck out and that's something I never do. If you want to stick yours out, you tell him. Let's face it, old boy, you probably started this.'

I stiffened.

'What the hell do you mean?'

'Now, don't get upset.' He grinned. 'You did tell me you let her off so she fell and hit her head, didn't you?'

I turned cold.

'I imagined she had come out of that.'

'Doesn't look as if she has, does it? Anyway, we'll know something with luck, after the specialist has seen her.'

'Does Vidal know?'

'Not yet, but he will have to be told. Fontane will call him sometime today.'

I moved to the door.

'Let me know what happens,' I said. 'It worries me that I could be responsible.'

'I wouldn't worry, old boy. If it wasn't you, it could be

121

someone else. After all, people are always snapping their fingers, aren't they?'

I went up to my office to find Connie already at her typewriter. We exchanged greetings and I looked through the briefs that had arrived. I was worried sick by what Dyer had told me. In an impulsive moment, I decided, no matter how great the risk, I had to see Val.

I gave Connie some work to do, told her I would be back in a few minutes and left the office. I looked down the long corridor that led to Val's bedroom. Then I walked fast to the door, paused, listened, heard nothing and tapped lightly. There was no reply to my tap.

With my heart pounding, I opened the door silently and looked into the room.

Alone, Val lay in the big bed.

'Val?'

Leaving the door ajar, I crossed the room to the bed and looked down at her. I received a shock. She looked so thin and white, and her fixed, blank stare frightened me.

'Val!'

She didn't move and her stare remained fixed.

I knew every second I remained in the room was dangerous. Any moment someone could come in and what excuse could I give for being there? If I had put her in this trance by snapping my fingers could I not get her out of it by snapping my fingers twice as Dyer had told me he had done? Dare I experiment with something I knew so little about?

'Val!'

Still no response.

I touched her arm.

Still no response.

I had to do it! I lifted my hand, hesitated, then snapped my fingers: once, twice.

Her reaction was immediate. She gave a convulsive shudder. Life came back into her eyes. She started up, staring at me.

'It's all right, darling ... it's me ... Clay.'

She reared back, her hands lifting and shaking.

'Val! It's me ... Clay!'

'You're not Clay!' Her voice was low: a croak. 'Get away

om me! I know who you are, you devil! Get away from me!'

The terror in her eyes, the terror in her croaking voice
rove me to the door.

'Get out!' Her voice was now shrill. 'Get out!'

Shaking, cold and shocked, I moved into the corridor and
uietly closed the door. I stood for some moments, leaning
gainst the wall, feeling sick and desperate. I had lost her!
he now imagined I was Vidal!

I walked unsteadily down the corridor, down the stairs
nd out to my car.

Once in the car, I tried to control myself. I sat there for
ome five minutes then, making the effort, I started the car
ngine.

I had to kill him!

But first to buy a gun!

*　　*　　*

got off the Turnpike on to East street and found parking
a lot behind a run down hotel. I walked north towards the
Harlem quarter. As I progressed I was aware of hostile stares.
didn't give a damn. I walked my way, shoving through the
lacks on the congested street, my eyes searching for a pawn
hop.

At the corner of Southern Beach road I found one. I
ushed open the double swing doors and walked into a big
pace that smelt of black people, dirty feet and despair.

Facing me was a long counter at which stood, in hopeless
esignation, some thirty or forty black men and women.
efore them on the counter were bundles which they clutched
ith possessive fear while three black clerks moved up and
own behind the counter with indifferent, arrogant expres-
ions.

I stood hesitating. Then I saw a black hand waving to me.
walked away from the counter to a small cubicle, boxed in
n either side but open at the back and front.

An old Negro in a black threadbare alpaca coat and a grey
annel shirt with a string tie smiled at me from behind the
ounter. He had a high domed forehead. His crinkly white

123

hair receded and his bushy white eyebrows made shades fo
his eyes.

'Yes, sir?' he said. 'There is something, sir?'

I moved close to him.

'I want to buy a gun,' I said.

What would he do? Send for the police? Refuse me?
was beyond caring.

'Yes, sir.' His expression conveyed I had asked for nothin
more ordinary than a flower vase or an alarm clock. 'A gun
Perhaps a sporting rifle, sir? We have a selection. I have a .2
rifle that has just come in. Would that be of interest, sir?'

'I want a pistol.' I wished I knew something about guns
'Not a rifle.'

He smiled, showing big yellow teeth like the keys of an ol
piano.

'Yes . . . so many people now want hand guns. It is the nev
way of life. We must protect ourselves. Certainly, sir, I ca
offer you something exceptional.' The black eyes moved ove
me, up and down, taking stock. 'The price comes a little high
but this gun is far from ordinary: a police .38 automatic:
beautiful weapon.'

I didn't know what to say. All I wanted was a gun capabl
of killing Vidal, but this I couldn't tell this old Negro.

'Well . . .'

'Would you be interested at one hundred and thirty dol
lars?' The black eyes stared fixedly at me. 'A beautifu
weapon, sir.'

'Show it to me.'

He went away and after several minutes, while I stood wit
my back to the shop, feeling curious eyes boring into me, he
came to the counter and laid a gun before me.

I stared down at it. It meant nothing to me. It was a gun
I felt a cold tremor run through me as I regarded the shor
barrel, the trigger and the blue metallic finish.

'You live in this neighbourhood, sir?' the old Negro asked
'It has become a sad district. Thirty years ago, I well remem
ber how pleasant it was. But now, people come to me ii
fear. They want guns. They need to protect themselves. Nov
with a gun like this . . . ' He picked up the gun and fondled it
'You could sleep peacefully. A knock on your door, the soun

f breaking glass, a shadow across your bed . . . with a gun like this you would feel secure.'

'I know nothing about guns,' I said huskily. 'Please show e.'

Ten minutes later, I walked out into the heat and the ind. For the first time in my life, I had a loaded gun in my p pocket.

I got back to the Vidal residence at 10.45. As I parked my ar I saw Dr Fontane and a short fat man I guessed would be e specialist coming down the steps from the house. They ere talking together. Fontane, bending forward, his bird-ke face worried, hanging on the words of the fat man. They ot in Fontane's car and drove away.

Dyer now appeared. Seeing me, he came down the steps nd joined me.

'Where have you been?' he asked.

'I had things to do. What's the news?'

'Foxed them both. The official verdict is a nervous break-own. These quacks! Anyway, Fontane has talked to Tiny. Ie's coming back.'

A sudden squall of rain and wind made him retreat up the teps and into the hall. I followed him. We both paused as ain poured out of the sky.

'Hell!' Dyer said. 'I think we're in for it. Did you hear the urricane warning half an hour ago?'

I couldn't care less about hurricanes.

'A nervous breakdown?'

He shrugged.

'That covers everything, doesn't it?' He was staring up at he now leaden sky. 'They say this is going to be the biggest low we have had since 1928. I'll have to see these lazy tykes et busy battening down.'

Nodding, he ran out into the rain and down the path owards his office.

Moving slowly, I mounted the stairs and walked into my ffice.

Connie was on the telephone, a half-eaten hamburger clutched in her fat little fingers.

'That's right,' she was saying. 'Okay, I'll fix the visas,' and he hung up. 'I've got one schedule tied up, Mr Burden,' she

125

said, smiling happily. 'I've sent Potter for the visas. They'r
for Mr and Mrs Lu Mayer.'

I didn't know what she was talking about nor did I care.
nodded.

'Good work,' I said. 'What else is there?'

'There is a schedule . . .'

I half listened. *He is coming back.* When? I had to know
I flicked down the switch of the intercom.

'Burden,' I said when Dyer answered. 'When did you sa
Mr Vidal was returning? Can I fix his reservation?'

'He is already on his way,' Dyer said. 'He's due in at 06.0
tomorrow. I've told his chauffeur. There's nothing for you t
handle.'

As I flicked up the switch, my gun hand went behind m
and my fingers touched the butt of the gun.

*   *   *

'Excuse me, Mr Burden,' Connie said, 'would you mind if
got the weather service?'

I was far away with my thoughts and came to with a start
I blinked at her.

'What was that again?'

She held up a tiny transistor.

'The weather service.'

'Oh, sure . . . go ahead.'

I looked across the big room to the two picture window
Rain poured down the big panes, blotting out the palm tree
and the sky.

The weather service man said that the hurricane, name
'Hermes', was coming from the West Indies, was approachin
the Florida coast at the rate of 20 miles an hour. Unless i
was diverted – which seemed unlikely – it would hit Key Wes
in two days' time and then Miami the following morning.

'This is a hurricane warning,' the voice said. 'Stand by fo
hourly reports.'

'What does all that mean?' I asked as Connie switched o
the transistor and produced a paper sack from her handbag

'When we get a hurricane warning, we have to mak
arrangements,' she told me. 'All the rich run away. People

ke you and me stick here and get battered. It's quite fun
eally. I've been through two hurricanes and I'm still here to
rag about it.' She peered into the paper sack. 'Would you
ancy a bit of choc. cake, Mr Burden?'

'Not right now, thank you,' I said.

The intercom buzzed. I flicked down the switch.

'Do you mind coming to my office, old boy?' Dyer said.
Bring an umbrella or something. It's raining like hell.'

'I'll be along and I can see it is raining.'

I got wet, running along the path to Dyer's office. I found
im at his desk, a telephone receiver clamped to his ear.

He was saying, 'Get men working on it, Harry. Board up
he place. You take care of the yacht . . . okay? What's that?
;od knows! You know Tiny. He could opt to stick. Yes . . .
all me back,' and he hung up.

I shook the rain off my jacket as I moved further into the
oom.

'Action stations.' He grinned. 'Hermes is going to be
iolent. From tomorrow the office closes. All the staff will
ither go to Dallas – that's Tiny's second headquarters or stay
ome. How about you, Burden? Want to stick around here or
o home?'

I rested a hip on his desk.

'I'm not with you. What's all the fuss?'

He laughed.

'Of course, you're from Boston. You haven't ever experi-
nced a hurricane. It's quite something. We bed down and sit
 out . . . those who have to. The migration of the rich, the
at and the powerful has already begun. Everyone who can
hoves off. Paradise City, Miami and Fort Lauderdale come
 a grinding halt. If Tiny opts to remain here, then Mrs
lements, the chef and the butler will stay.' He pulled a face.
Me too. I've been through this caper before. It's pretty
reary. Canned food, no electricity, hellish noise, but plenty
f booze. What do you want to do? You'd better stay home.
here will be no work to do.'

'You mean everything literally comes to a standstill?'

'That's what I'm telling you. According to the weather
ureau Hermes is going to be a real sonofabitch. Your best
et is to stay home.'

127

'What is going to happen to Mrs Vidal?'

He shrugged.

'That's for Tiny to decide. If he thinks she shouldn't b[e] moved then I'll have to stay here. When he arrives tomorro[w] I'm hoping he'll have her shifted to Dallas. I want to kno[w] where you will be. As soon as Hermes blows itself out, I'[ll] have to recall the staff. I have your home address, haven't I[?]'

I didn't hesitate.

'I'll stick around here,' I said. 'If things get rugged I migh[t] be of help, but if Vidal goes to Dallas, I'll go home.'

He looked surprised.

'Please yourself. You won't have anything to do, but if yo[u] want to stay, it'll be company for me. Bring an overnight ba[g] with you tomorrow. After tomorrow no one will be happy o[n] the streets.'

A crash of thunder rattled the windows.

'It's building up.' He reached for the telephone. 'Have [a] word with Mrs Clements. She'll fix your room here.'

It was now raining so violently I had to borrow an um[-] brella from the receptioness before returning to the house. [I] told Connie not to come in tomorrow and I would call he[r] when the hurricane had blown itself out. I then called Mr[s] Clements on the intercom.

'Mr Dyer suggests I have a room here until the hurrican[e] is over,' I said. 'Can that be arranged?'

'Yes, Mr Burden. Room 2, next to your office.'

That put me thirty yards from Val's room.

There was very little work now to keep us occupied. Around 16.00, as there was a lull in the rain, I sent Conni[e] home.

When she had gone, I lit a cigarette and leaned back in m[y] chair. So Vidal was returning tomorrow. Val was supposed t[o] be having a nervous breakdown. I was going to spend th[e] following night here, close to her and close to Vidal.

I took the gun from my hip pocket and examined it. Th[e] old Negro had explained about the safety catch, had show[n] me how to load and unload it. It was now unloaded. I ha[d] six cartridges in my pocket. I raised the gun, sighted along th[e] short barrel and squeezed the trigger. The hammer made [a] sharp snapping sound. I wondered if when the time came [I] could bring myself to shoot. I put the gun in my brief case and lit another cigarette. Now was the time to think of a safe and foolproof method to kill Vidal. No one must suspect Val nor me. I sat in the stillness of the room with the sound of the storm for the next two hours while I racked my brains but no foolproof idea presented itself. I tried to assure myself that an opportunity would arrive. I had a gun. When the opportunity did arrive, I would use the gun. That was as far as I got with my thinking: a pretty feeble effort which depressed me.

Finally, I quit thinking and left the office. The wind was now screaming through the palm trees. Driving towards home, I found the traffic was bad. All cars seemed to be heading out of the city. There were many buses crammed with old people. As Dyer had said the migration had begun.

Along the main shopping street, men were busy removing electric signs and boarding up shop windows. A string of trucks piled high with bedding and cooking utensils held me up, and impatiently I took a side road that would take me in a circular route to my complex.

In the residential quarter I saw men standing on bungalow roofs capping chimneys and others plugging windows and door crevices.

The wind was so violent I had trouble in steering my car in a straight course. Every now and then a gust forced the Plymouth half across the street.

I was glad to drive down the ramp of the communal garage and get out of the wind. As I locked the car, torrential rain began to fall.

Leaving the elevator, I walked into the apartment. Rhoda was standing by the window, looking out at the rain and the wind lashed palms.

'So the hurricane is going to arrive after all,' I said as I put my brief case, containing the gun, in my desk drawer. 'Did you see all the preparations going on?'

She didn't turn nor speak. I frowned at her back, then shrugging, I went into the bedroom.

A suitcase lay on the bed. I paused, then crossing to the bed, I lifted the lid of the suitcase. The case contained a jumble of Rhoda's clothes. She was the most god-awful

129

packer and when we went away, I packed for her.

I returned to the living room.

'What's the idea of the suitcase, honey?' I asked, feeling suddenly uneasy.

'I'm staying at the hotel until the hurricane is over.' Her voice was flat and cold and she didn't turn around. 'Daphne (she was Rhoda's boss) says we shall be busy as the old cow will have nothing to do except buy things. She says the streets won't be safe, so I'm moving in, if it's of any interest to you.'

The stiff way she was holding herself, the tone of her voice increased my uneasiness.

'Is something biting you, honey?'

She turned. Her face was flushed and her eyes were snapping.

'I have something to show you, you two faced jerk!' she exclaimed. She ran to the table and picked up a copy of *Vogue*, turned back at a full page coloured photograph. She thrust it at me. Even upside down as she held it in her shaking hand I could see it was a photograph of Val.

I kept my face expressionless.

'What's so unusual about that?' I said.

'Don't try to con me, you sonofabitch!' Rhoda screamed. 'I showed this to Bill Olson and who do you think he said it was: your gorgeous, efficient Val Dart! The tart you have been mooning about for six goddamn years! The whore you went away with, getting what she wouldn't give you six years ago! You and your cheap diamond and emerald ring!'

She threw something at me. It struck my face and fell to the floor. I saw it was the box containing the engagement ring I had so hopefully bought Val so many years ago and which I had kept as I had thought safely at the back of my shirt drawer. With the ring, I had kept Val's letters.

I picked up the box and put it in my pocket. A crash of thunder rattled the windows.

'You dared to hit me, you stinker, when I said you were screwing that whore and you were screwing her all the time! You pick nose bastard! You . . . you . . . ' She rushed at me, her fingers like claws. I caught her wrists and pushed her gently but firmly into a chair.

'All right, Rhoda, relax. Let's talk about it. Let's cut out

130

he screaming and the name calling,' I said quietly. 'I want a ivorce.'

She was struggling to get up, but when I said that she went mp and stared up at me.

'You want . . . what?'

'A divorce. Let's be civilised about this, Rhoda. You must dmit we don't get along. We shouldn't have married. You now as well as I do that this is a fact. You are young. You'll nd someone who will make you much happier than I do.'

She drew in a shuddering breath.

'Are you planning to marry that bitch once you get rid of 1e?' she demanded, her voice thick with rage.

'I have no plans, Rhoda. I just want to be free, and I think ou should also be free.'

'Do you?' Her lips twisted into a sneer. 'How very con-iderate of you! So you divorce me and you'll be free to screw hat bitch whenever she feels like it. That's the idea, isn't it?'

'Rhoda. Can't we discuss this reasonably? I am asking you r a divorce for the good of both of us. Right now you are pset, but when this hurricane is over, when you are in a almer mood, think about it. I am sure you will realise that : is as much to your advantage as it is to mine.'

'Is that right? How nice to know! Let me tell you, Mr ¶ot-pants, I don't have to think about it! I've already 1ought about it!' She got to her feet and marched into the edroom.

Feeling cold and sick I went to the window and stared out t the storm.

She came back, carrying her suitcase. She had put on a 1ac and a plastic rain hat. She looked very immature and retty as she dumped the case on my desk and faced me.

'Now I'm going to give you something to think about, my ashing Casanova. When this hurricane has blown itself out, shall come back here still as your wife! In the meantime, ou will tell Mr Henry Vidal that you are not going to work r him any longer. You will go to Massingham and ask for our job back. You do that and I'll forget your dirty little ambol in sex. From now on, you are going to make me happy 1stead of that whore. You are not getting a divorce! I'm atisfied as I am. Get all that?'

131

'I'm sorry, Rhoda. I want out and I am having out. I
don't want to live with you any more. If you won't give me
a divorce, then we must each go our own ways,' I said quietly

'How wrong can you be! And I'll tell you for why. If you
don't do what I have said – quit working for Mr Money-bags
Vidal, quit sniffing around that slinky bitch, then I will write
to Mr Money-bags and tell him what you are up to. I've seen
photos of him. He's no cry baby. When he learns you have
been screwing his wife, he'll give you the beating you deserve
and he'll give her one too. So watch it! You quit by the time
I get back or you will land in hospital and don't come snivelling to me. I won't care!'

She picked up her suitcase and left the apartment. The
bang of the door coincided with a crash of thunder.

Eight

THE BELL of my alarm clock which I had set to go off at 06.00 woke me with a start. I had gone to bed early and knowing wouldn't be able to sleep with so much on my mind I had taken three sleeping pills.

Before the pills had finally bludgeoned me into sleep I had looked at my future with despair. I was sure Rhoda was capable of writing to Vidal. Val had said with conviction that if ever Vidal found out we were lovers he would have us killed. I was sure now this was no idle warning. There was no use in confiding in Rhoda, telling her that if she gave me away I could be killed. She would only think this was an exaggeration to prevent her telling him. She just wouldn't believe it: a beating, yes, but murder, no.

Murder?

This brought me full circle. If I killed Vidal my troubles would be over. Val would be free and Rhoda could no longer blackmail me. Even if Rhoda refused me a divorce, Val and I could go away. Once Val was back to her old efficient self, we could work together. We could disappear to Canada or to England. With our training and experience we were certain to get good jobs in some travel office and later (who knows?) by saving our money, we might even set up as travel agents on our own.

Under the drowsy influence of the sleeping pills I became more optimistic. Maybe the future wasn't going to be so black as I had first thought. As I lay there in this half-world of sleep and wakefulness I even felt capable of murdering Vidal.

I struggled up and turned off the alarm. The sun was

shining through the blinds. Sitting on the edge of the bed I ran my fingers through my hair, grimacing as my head began to throb and ache. The strange silence in the room puzzled me. It was as if I had become suddenly deaf, then I realised the wind had died down. For the past twelve hours it screaming and the noise of the wind-lashed palm trees had been deafening. I went to the window and drew up the blind.

Outside, everything dripped water, but there was no wind and the sun felt strong.

Maybe, I thought, the hurricane has already blown itself out.

It seemed strange to have the apartment to myself and not to hear Rhoda singing in the bathroom. Loneliness is a funny thing. When I had her around, she irritated me, but now, I missed her.

I made coffee and then dressed. At 07.15 I went down to the garage.

Hank, the night man, was polishing a car. He was a tall, thin black who took too much interest in the occupants of the apartments.

'Morning, Mr Burden,' he said, grinning. 'You're right early. I see Mrs Burden's car ain't here.'

'She's staying at the hotel and I'm staying at Paradise Largo until the hurricane passes. Hold any mail for us, will you, Hank?'

'Sure will, Mr Burden. That hurricane is going to be a big nuisance.'

'Looks as if it has already blown itself out.'

Grinning, he shook his head.

'No, sir. That little hurricane ain't blown itself out. It's gathering its strength. By dusk, it'll really get going.

I drove out on to the empty streets. The City now looked as if it were expecting a hostile invasion. The windows of the stores and better shops were boarded up. There was scarcely any traffic. Coming to the hotel belt I saw men trimming the palms and sawing off overhanging tree branches.

The security guard nodded to me as I showed him my pass.

'I'll be staying until it's over,' I told him.

He grunted, his expression surly.

'So will I if this goddamn box doesn't blow away.'

'Has Mr Vidal arrived yet?'

'Passed through half an hour ago.'

I found a change in the house when I parked my car. All the windows were boarded up and there were two men on the flat roof, capping the chimneys. A Chinese gardener was staking the standard rose trees. Another was shoring up a leaning palm.

Entering my dark office, I turned on the lights. On my desk stood a hurricane lamp and a box of matches. I glanced at the boarded up windows, then at my desk clock. The time was 08.00.

Henriques, Vidal's accountant, had asked me to prepare the month's statement giving names, destinations and costs. As I had nothing else to do and needed to keep my mind occupied I got out the various dockets and receipts and began to list them.

Around 08.45 a tap came on the door and Dyer came in.

'Hello there.' He had a powerful electric torch in his hand which he placed on my desk. 'The hurricane is supposed to hit around 21.00. All electricity will be cut off so you'd better keep this handy. It's going to be damned hot without the air conditioners and with no ventilation.' He sat on the corner of my desk and lit a cigarette. 'Tiny arrived about an hour ago.' He grimaced. 'Not in the best of tempers. He's with Mrs V. now.'

'Did he say if they were going to stay?'

Dyer grinned.

'He didn't even say good morning. I'm working in the room immediately below this one. His office is next to mine at the back, overlooking the pool in case he yells for you. There's a lot of mail come in, probably the last until it's over.'

'Anything I can do?'

'Not right now. My intercom is four. See you,' and he left me.

I sat still, wondering what was going on in Val's room. My nerves were jumpy and I had a sick feeling in my stomach. I opened my desk drawer where I had put my brief case. The outline of the gun gave me no comfort. Shutting the drawer, I tried to concentrate on the dockets, but my mind kept chasing down the corridor to Val's room.

Then remembering I had left my overnight bag in the Plymouth, I got to my feet and went to the door, opened it and stood listening. I heard nothing. Slowly, I moved along the corridor to within ten yards of Val's door. I paused at the head of the stairs and again listened.

Suddenly I heard Vidal's short barking laugh. The sound chilled me.

'You'd better get up.' His squeaky voice came clearly to me. 'Does you more harm than good lolling around in bed. Get dressed and find something to do!'

Seeing the door handle turn, I started swiftly down the stairs. I reached the hall as Vidal reached the head of the stairs.

'Ah, Burden!'

His voice stopped me as if I had run into a wall. I turned and looked up at him. He was wearing a pearl grey City suit with a white silk shirt and a blood red tie. He came swiftly down the stairs and as he passed me, he went on, 'I want to talk to you.' There was a heavy frown on his face and as he walked, he slapped his hands together impatiently.

Following him, I was again aware of the power and width of his shoulders that seemed to ooze strength.

He opened a door and bounced into a vast room, dominated by a big Chippendale desk: a room of comfort, luxury and good taste. He went around the desk and sat down.

'I'm pleased you are staying, Burden. You never know . . . you could be useful. I have to stay: an important telephone call. Mrs Vidal has elected to stay with me. God knows why.' He shrugged impatiently. 'She would be better leaving with Mrs Clements. She says she doesn't feel like the journey.' He waved to a chair. 'Sit down.'

As I sat down there came a tap on the door and the butler came in with a tray of coffee which he set on the desk.

'Want coffee?' Vidal asked me.

'No, thank you.' I felt I would throw up if I took coffee. 'I've had mine.'

'Right.' He waved the butler away. 'Harris, you'd better get going. Guilio will look after me.'

'Very good, sir.' The butler closed the door after him.

'They're all nervous,' Vidal said. 'I dislike having nervous people around me.' He paused, then went on, 'Your work's very satisfactory, Burden. It couldn't have been easy with Mrs Vidal having the vapours. Have you got a secretary?'

'Yes, but I told her to keep away until the hurricane's over.'

'Mrs Vidal, as I expected, doesn't want to continue working with you. She found it too hard so you'd better keep this girl you've found if you're satisfied with her. What are we paying her?'

I told him.

'That's all right. Now I have a job for you. Get on to it right away. If this hurricane turns out as bad as they say it's going to be, we'll lose the telephone: all the lines will be down. Charter an air taxi on stand-by to be ready to take off the moment the weather permits. Destination San Salvador, three passengers with luggage. I'll give you the names later, but get the aircraft booked.' He gave a mirthless grin. 'Tell that jerk I'll pay cash.'

'Yes, Mr Vidal.' I got to my feet.

'Don't run away for the moment. When you've done that, Burden, do me a favour, will you?'

This was so unexpected, I stared at him for a moment before saying, 'Of course, Mr Vidal.'

'Keep Mrs Vidal amused this afternoon, will you? She gets along with you. Play gin rummy or some goddamn thing with her. She's nervy and I have a load of work to do.'

I could scarcely believe I was hearing rightly.

'It'll be my pleasure,' I said huskily.

'That's a good fellow.' He reached for a legal looking document. It was his way of dismissing me.

My heart thumping with excitement, I moved into the hall, shutting Vidal's door gently behind me. Coming down the stairs was Mrs Clements, Harris, the butler and a fat man I assumed was the chef. They were all carrying suitcases. I stood aside to let them pass. Mrs Clements gave me a curt nod, Harris inclined his head, the chef ignored me. When they had left the house, I went into Dyer's office.

He was thumping a typewriter with two fingers. He paused to grin at me.

'The rats gone?'

'Where are they off to?'

'Catching the last flight to Dallas. They've all got the jitters about Hermes. Tiny told them to go and we now have no staff except Gesetti. He swears he can cook. I hope he can. You'll have to make your own bed. Can you type?'

'Fair.'

'You could help out.' He pushed some papers across his desk. 'If you will type this lot with two copies I'll be obliged.'

'Sure.' I took the papers up to my office, put them on the desk, hesitated, then started from the office towards Val's room. I had only taken three steps along the corridor when I came to an abrupt halt.

Coming up the stairs, moving like a ghost, was Gesetti.

We looked at each other. From under the brim of his white hat, his flat snake's eyes glittered menacingly.

The sight of him chilled me.

'Looking for something, buster?' he demanded and came up the last of the stairs with the speed of a cat.

I backed away from him. He looked as lethal as a cobra. Panic grabbed me. I backed into my office and hurriedly shut the door.

This was the man, Val had told me, who would kill us if Vidal found out that we were lovers. He put the fear of God into me. It was something I couldn't control. I was furious with myself that I had shown him so clearly I was frightened of him, but there was something so vicious and deadly about him surely anyone would be frightened of him?

I sat at my desk, wiping my clammy hands with my handkerchief, listening for the sound of his footsteps, but hearing nothing. I was sure he was still outside my door. I had to restrain the urge to rush to the door and turn the key.

It took me nearly ten minutes to calm down. I now hadn't the courage to venture out of the office. I still couldn't be sure that Gesetti wasn't out there in the corridor so I called Roger Everet of the Florida Air Taxi service.

'Hello, Burden,' he said when he came to the telephone. 'What's it this time? Your dwarf paid up like a lamb by the way.'

'He wants an air taxi: three passengers and luggage for

138

an Salvador on stand-by. As soon as Hermes has blown itself
ut, he wants to take off.'

'Can do. Same terms?'

'Same terms.'

'Okay, tell him the kite will be at readiness.'

'What do the weather boys say?'

'Could be through in three or four days but it'll be bad
vhile it lasts. Let's see, today's Tuesday. He could take off
aturday with luck.'

'Okay. I'll tell him.'

I still had no desire to see Val as yet. Gesetti had acted
ike a bucket of cold water thrown over me so I began to type
he paper Dyer had given me: dull speeches of directors of
n oil corporation.

As I typed, I became aware that the wind was rising. The
alm trees began to rustle. Away in the distance came the
aint rumble of thunder.

* * *

At lunch time I went down to the darkened dining room. On
he table were two plates of sandwiches and bottles of beer.
. took two sandwiches and a beer back to my office, then
:ompleted the work Dyer had given me.

The wind was now whistling through the trees and slamming against the boarded up windows. The thunder sounded
:loser.

Later, Dyer called me on the intercom.

'Finished those speeches yet?' he asked.

'Yes. Shall I bring them down?'

'Tiny's asking for them. Take them to him, will you?'

I found Vidal at his desk, a pint of milk and some sandwiches near him. He looked up from the paper he was
reading.

'Those speeches you wanted, Mr Vidal,' I said and put
them on his desk.

'Thanks.' He leaned back in his chair and reached for a
sandwich. 'Got that air taxi fixed?'

'Yes. Everet thinks you could take off on Saturday.'

'I hope he's right. Now go talk to Mrs Vidal. I've just been up. She's complaining she's lonely.' He eyed me, then went on, 'and listen, Burden, don't give her any sympathy. She imagines she is having a nervous breakdown. That's a lot of hooey. She's just bored. When women get bored they dream up any damn thing to make themselves the centre of attention. So don't play along with her. Understand?'

I hesitated. Then bracing myself, I looked directly at him.

'Excuse me, Mr Vidal, but I don't agree.'

He was reaching for a pen as I spoke. His hand hovered over the pen and he looked up sharply.

'What was that?'

'I was with Mrs Vidal when she fainted. She hurt her head. Dr Fontane visited her twice a day for three days and he called in a specialist. It doesn't seem reasonable to me to suggest this is an attempt to attract attention.'

He sat back, his little eyes probing.

'Interesting. Do you think she is having a nervous breakdown, Burden?'

'I don't know, but you don't fall and hurt your head for the fun of it.'

He gave his short barking laugh.

'That tells me how much you know about women. Of course they'll fall and hurt their heads or scratch their wrists with a razor blade or take just enough sleeping pills if they feel neglected. Women are special animals, but I understand them. Don't worry about Mrs Vidal. If anyone is to worry it'll be me and I'm not worrying yet. Go and see her, amuse her, do something to get her mind off herself.' He reached for his pen and signed the paper he had been reading.

I remained where I was. He looked up and frowned at me.

'Go along, Burden. I'm busy.'

'I think you should begin to worry, Mr Vidal.' I was determined now to have it out with him. 'I think there is something radically wrong with Mrs Vidal.

That made him pause. He sat back in his chair.

'Wrong? What do you mean?'

'There are times when she appears to be hypnotised.'

His eyebrows crawled up.

'Hypnotised? What the hell are you saying? Who would

140

vant to hypnotise her?' He gave his short, barking laugh. 'Utter nonsense!'

This made me angry and without caring, I said, 'I believe you are responsible! I believe you have hypnotised her!'

He stared fixedly at me, his little eyes glittering. Then the telephone bell rang. He waved me to the door.

'Believe that, Burden, you'll believe anything. Now get out!' He picked up the telephone receiver.

As I closed the door, I heard him say, 'This is Vidal. Goddamn it! You're late . . . '

Well, I've told him, I thought as I climbed the stairs. He now knows I know. Would that make him more cautious? Would it make it now easier for Val? That was all I wanted: to make it easier for her.

Reaching the head of the stairs, I walked quickly down the corridor and tapped on Val's door.

'Who is it?' Her voice sounded unsteady.

'It's Clay,' I said, my mouth close to the door panel.

The key turned and the door opened. Val moved back as I entered the room.

We looked at each other as I shut the door. She had on a blue housecoat. Her hair lay on her shoulders. The sight of her, so pale, dark smudges under her eyes, her hands trembling sent a pang through me.

'How do you feel, darling?' I longed to take her in my arms.

'How do I feel?' She moved listlessly to a chair and sank into it. 'Desperate, Clay. I don't know what I'm going to do. I have no more will. I want to kill myself.' Her face crumbled and she closed her eyes. 'I haven't even the will to do that.'

A sudden crash of thunder made me start. The wind now was screaming around the house.

'Kill yourself?' I turned cold with alarm. 'What's happened, Val? Has he molested you?'

'Oh, there's that.' She put her hands to her face. 'I've got beyond caring about that. No, it's the end of everything now for me and for you. He has decided to leave. I am to go with him.'

'Leave? Where is he going?'

'He has decided to settle in Lima . . . where he can't be extradited.'

I pulled up a chair close to her and sat down.

'Extradited? Val, darling, don't talk in riddles. Is he i
trouble?'

She nodded.

'You were right, Clay. His empire is going to crash. H
owes millions and the Federal people are investigating h
tax position. He doesn't seem to mind. He treats it as a joke
As soon as the hurricane is over, he, I and Gesetti are flying t
San Salvador where he has hidden money. Then we go t
Lima. He says he'll begin again. It also means he can neve
return to the United States. I go with him. I can never return
I'll lose you again, but this time for good.'

I couldn't believe this. I caught hold of her hand.

'I won't let him take you, Val! I said I would help you and
I'm going to help you! I'll tell the tax people he is preparing
to skip. They'll arrest him!'

She shook her head.

'It's too late to do that. He is protected by his lawyers
Before the Federal people could get a warrant, he'll be gone
taking me with him. No . . . that's not the way.' She stood up
abruptly and began to move around the room. 'There is no
way . . .'

A violent gust of wind slammed against the house followed
by a crash of thunder. I could hear the rain beating on the
roof.

I thought of the gun in my desk drawer.

'I have a gun, Val.'

She paused to stare at me, her eyes widening.

'A gun?'

'When he is dead you will be free.'

She put her hand to her throat.

'I can never be free – even when he is dead.' A crazed
expression came into her eyes. 'Shoot me!' Her voice turned
shrill. 'That is the solution! If only you knew how tired I am
of living the life he has forced me to live. If I had the will, I
would beg you to give me the gun and I would do it myself.'
She came up to me, laying her hand on my arm. 'You can do
it, Clay! Shoot me in the head! They will think it is suicide.
No one would blame you, darling! Don't you see? You would
be freeing me! Please say you will do it!'

142

I looked at her in horror.

God! I thought. He has driven her out of her mind!

Her fingers were digging into my arm as she went on, 'No
ne will hear the shot in this storm! The doctors know I am
n the verge of a breakdown! You will be safe, darling. No
ne would suspect you. Get the gun now! Then do it . . .
lease! No one will suspect you!'

'Val! For God's sake, pull yourself together!' I had to raise
my voice against the noise of the storm which was beginning
to become deafening. 'I'm not doing it! Now, stop it! Pull
ourself together! There must be some way out for us!'

She let go of my arm and stepped back. The misery in her
yes sickened me.

'I thought you loved me! How can you love me and let me
uffer like this . . . oh, go away!' She ran to the bed and threw
erself face down on it. As she began to sob there came a
remendous crashing sound as if a tree had been uprooted
nd had fallen against the house.

I went to her and put my hands on her shoulders.

'Darling Val! Please don't. I said I would help you and I
will help you. Please be patient.'

She rounded on me, her face convulsed with anger and
ear.

'Go away! I hate you! Leave me! Go away!' Her voice rose
o a scream. Fearing that even above the noise of the
lements raging outside someone might hear her, I backed to
he door, hesitated, then moved into the corridor.

I stood for some moments listening to her wild sobbing,
hen unable to bear the sound, I closed the door and made my
ay unsteadily back to my office.

The noise of the hurricane beat against my skull. I went to
my desk chair and sat down, holding my hands against my
ars, feeling as if I were going demented.

I had to do something! I had no alternative now if I wasn't
oing to lose her! I had to kill Vidal!

A grinding sound, followed by the sound of splintering
ood coming from downstairs brought me to my feet. Then
my door slammed open by a violent gust of wind that swept
my desk clear of papers, overturned my desk lamp and threw
wo of my telephones to the floor.

143

'Burden!!'

Vidal's voice bawled from below.

I reached the corridor, bracing myself against the wind that roared up the stairs. I started down them, hanging on the banister rail. I was stunned by the force of the wind which was howling through the open front door.

I could see Vidal and Dyer struggling to get the door closed.

The hall with its big oil paintings and its suits of armour was a shambles. Four of the big pictures had been blown of their hooks, two of the suits of armour were in pieces.

Lying in the middle of the floor was Gesetti, blood on his face, an oil painting in a heavy frame on top of him.

Stepping around him, I struggled across the hall and joined the two men wrestling with the door. With my added weight, we got it shut.

'Wedge it!' Vidal snapped. 'Use one of those pikes.'

Dyer released his hold on the door and dashed to pick up a pike that had fallen from the wall. As soon as his weight was removed, the door slammed open again, sending Vidal and myself sprawling. Another struggle began to shut the door. Not only the wind but the rain hammered us and by the time we got the door shut and jammed into place by the pike we were all soaked.

Gesetti groaned and tried to sit up. Dyer went to him and supported him. I couldn't touch him. He gave me the horrors. Vidal joined Dyer and they got Gesetti to his feet. He shook his head, spraying blood, blinked and straightened up.

'I'm okay, boss,' he muttered but he leaned heavily on Dyer.

'I'll take care of him,' Vidal said. 'You two clean up the mess.'

Catching hold of Gesetti he led him down the corridor towards the back of the house.

'Phew!' Dyer wiped his dripping face with the back of his hand. 'Did you bring a change?'

'Yes.'

'We'll get out of these wet things and then get this mess fixed. This is the worst goddamn hurricane I've run into, and it'll last for at least another four days.'

We went up the stairs and separated at our rooms. It took me only a few minutes to strip off, dry myself and put on a sweat shirt and slacks. I was down in the hall stacking the oil paintings against the wall when Dyer joined me in an open neck shirt and hipsters.

'The telephone's gone,' he said as we began to carry the bits of armour into a small reception room. 'The electricity will go any moment now.'

I saw he had a powerful torch stuck in his belt.

Vidal appeared, still dripping.

'How is he, sir?' Dyer asked as Vidal started up the stairs.

'Not so good . . . concussion I guess.' Vidal paused. 'How are you enjoying yourself, Burden?' He gave his barking laugh. 'A bit of a change from Boston, huh?'

I stood silent, hating him.

He turned to Dyer.

'I've told him to stay in bed. Let him be. I've given him a couple of pills. With luck he'll be all right tomorrow. You'd better take care of the supper. You help him, Burden.' He started up the stairs two at a time and disappeared along the corridor.

I looked at my watch. The time was 17.50. The afternoon seemed to be going on forever.

'Let's finish this, then we'll inspect the kitchen,' Dyer said. 'I could do with a drink, couldn't you?'

It took us only a few minutes to complete what we had begun, then we went along to the kitchen.

Dyer inspected the big refrigerator.

'Plenty of cold cuts,' he said with satisfaction. 'Cans galore . . at least we won't starve.'

Going to another cupboard, he found the liquor store.

'Whisky?'

'I guess.'

He built two big whiskies, added ice and saluted me.

While all this was going on the rain and the wind lashed the house and thunder crashed. The noise was infernal.

I felt steadier after the drink. My mind kept going to Val.

'While we have the light,' Dyer said when he had finished his drink, 'suppose we check the doors and windows. We don't want another blow in like that one.'

145

We found one of the doors leading to the garden unsafe. Dyer found wood, hammer and nails and we shored up the door. By the time we had checked the windows and repaired three of them it was getting on for 19.00.

'I'm hungry,' Dyer said. 'Feel like eating?'

'No . . . I'll have another drink though.'

While I was fixing the drinks, Dyer made himself a beer sandwich.

'How about Mrs Vidal?' he asked with his mouth full. 'Maybe she wants something.'

'You finish that. I'll go up and ask her.'

Feeling light headed after the two big whiskies, I mounted the stairs and started down the corridor. Then I paused. Vidal was coming out of Val's room. He had changed into a scarlet open neck shirt and white slacks. Humming under his breath, he closed and locked the door. Leaving the key in the lock he started towards me, his little eyes narrowing.

'Yes, Burden?'

'I – I was wondering if Mrs Vidal would like some supper,' I said.

'Very thoughtful. No . . . we'll let her be for a while. She is being a little dramatic.' He laughed. 'I find it is better to leave women alone when they become tiresome. Women dislike being ignored.' He took hold of my arm. His fingers felt like steel hooks. 'Suppose you get me something, Burden, if it is not too much trouble . . . a few sandwiches and lots of coffee.' He steered me to the head of the stairs. 'Put it in my office, will you?'

I jerked away from his grip. His touch was to me the touch of a leper.

He smiled.

'Don't worry about Mrs Vidal, Burden. I have a little spare time now, so I will do the worrying should it be necessary.'

He stared at me, his eyes hostile, then moving into his bedroom, he closed the door gently in my face.

*   *   *

'Hi, Burden!'

I looked down the well of the staircase. Dyer was beckoning to me.

'What is it?' I was in no mood for his company.

'Come on down.'

No excuse came to my mind, so reluctantly I descended the stairs. He moved back into the kitchen.

'Does she want anything?' he asked as I followed him into the kitchen.

'Vidal says no.' I couldn't disguise the bitterness in my voice. 'He's locked her in.'

'He treats her like a puppet.' Dyer shrugged. 'Never mind about her, Burden. You and I have problems. Shut the door and keep your voice down.'

I looked sharply at him. There was a worried, uneasy expression on his face. As I closed the door, he began to build two whiskies.

'Vidal wants food,' I said.

'It's all fixed. Are you sure you don't want anything?'

'Nothing. What problems?'

He lifted his hand while he listened.

'He's coming down now. I'll take him his supper. Then we can talk.'

Picking up a tray of sandwiches and a jug of coffee, he left the kitchen. I moved around restlessly, nursing the whisky until he returned. He shut the door.

'We're off duty,' he said. 'Orders not to be disturbed.' He came close to me and keeping his voice low, he asked, 'How are you fixed, Burden, if you lost your job?'

I stared at him blankly.

'All right. I can go back to the A.T.S. Do you think I'm going to lose it?'

'It's more than likely. I'll lose mine too and I haven't a job waiting for me.'

'What makes you think we're going to lose our jobs?'

'Strictly between you and me, old boy, Tiny's in real trouble. While he was upstairs with Mrs V. I went into his office with some papers he wanted. On his desk was a letter from Jason Shackman, his attorney: a tip off that the Feds are on to him for tax evasion and they're applying for a warrant. Shackman says he hasn't a hope and he had better get out and fast. He has a bolt hole in Lima. They couldn't get at him there, but who the hell wants to live in Lima?'

'He's booked an air taxi to San Salvador.'

Dyer pulled a face.

'There goes my job. He hasn't a lot of money. He . . .'

'But he's worth millions!' I broke in.

Dyer shook his head.

'He had millions but not now. He was crazy enough to have financed a deal with the Libyans and they took him to the cleaners.' He glanced uneasily at the kitchen door. 'This is strictly confidential, old boy. I shouldn't be telling you this. He owes the tax people a hell of a sum. He's in real trouble. Know what I think? After living the way he has – the best of everything – Lima could be his end.'

'What do you mean?' I was now listening intently.

'It would never surprise me if he put a bullet through his head. Tiny's a bit unbalanced. He's fine when he's living it up, but yellow when the crunch comes. I could be wrong, but that's my bet.'

I thought about this, then shook my head.

'I can't imagine him killing himself,' I said. 'No . . . not Vidal.'

Dyer shrugged.

'You don't know him as I do. You could be right, but it wouldn't surprise me if his nerve broke and he opted for out.' He finished his drink. 'I thought I'd tell you what's in the wind. I've always had a feeling my job was too good to last.' He grinned ruefully. 'I've managed to put a little money by for the rainy day, but not much.'

I was only half listening to what he was saying. A sudden idea was growing in my mind.

'Well, I guess I'll go up. I have some thinking to do.' Dyer moved to the door. 'We should be all right tonight . . . touch wood. If you hear anything alarming come arunning. See you,' and he left me.

I stood for some minutes, listening to the storm raging outside, then picking up the bottle of whisky and taking my glass I walked quietly up the stairs and into my office. As

148

ut the bottle and glass on my desk, the lights in the room
ickered and went out.

The torch Dyer had left was right by my hand. I groped
or it, found it and switched it on. I went quickly into the
orridor. Vidal came bouncing up the stairs, torch in hand.

'All right, Burden,' he said. 'I'll take care of Mrs Vidal.
ou take care of yourself.'

Dyer's door opened and he came to the doorway, holding a
urricane lamp.

'I'll take that,' Vidal said, taking the lamp from Dyer. 'Go
own and light my lamps, will you?' He went on to Val's
oor, unlocked it and entered, leaving the door ajar.

'It's a wonder the lights haven't gone before this,' Dyer
aid and using his torch, he hurried down the stairs to Vidal's
ffice.

I stood looking down the corridor at Val's door, feeling a
urge of bitter frustration that Vidal had gone to her and not
.

'There is nothing to be alarmed about, Valerie,' I heard
Vidal say curtly. 'Here's a light. Perhaps you had better go to
ed instead of sitting there and please no more dramatics.'

I heard Val stifle a sob. The sound was like a knife thrust
o me.

'Please stop snivelling,' Vidal said impatiently. 'Do you
want something to eat?'

'Leave me alone.' Her voice was low and muffled.

'Please yourself.' He backed out of the room. I hurriedly
stepped into my office and stood out of sight until I heard
him go down the stairs. Then I moved out into the corridor
as Dyer came up.

'I'll turn in,' he said, 'not that anyone can sleep in this
infernal racket.'

'Have you looked at Gesetti?' I asked.

'No. I've forgotten about him. Maybe I'd better take a
look.'

'I'll go. Where is he?'

'Fourth door on the lower corridor. See you,' and he went
into his bedroom.

I stood listening, but only the sound of the screaming wind
and the rain came to me. I braced myself and went silently

down the stairs, past Vidal's door, along the corridor until I reached Gesetti's door. I listened. Gesetti was snoring: a massive, grunting noise a pig would make. I looked up and down the corridor, turned the handle and peered into the darkness. Then screening the bulb with my fingers, I directed the beam of the torch on to the bed.

Gesetti lay on his back, the sheet up to his chin, a big piece of plaster on his forehead. He slept, his mouth open, his snores reverberating around the room.

Satisfied I had nothing to fear from him, I closed the door and returned to my office. I lit the hurricane lamp and sat at my desk.

The foolproof plan to kill Vidal which had up to now completely eluded me was now clear in my mind. Both Val and Dyer had unwittingly presented it to me.

Without their information the idea would never have occurred to me. How simple it was!

The facts were that Vidal was ruined, a warrant for his arrest was imminent, he had lost his millions and he was faced with exile in Lima.

Those were incontestable facts that would stand up under police scrutiny.

To these facts add the noise of the hurricane, his hopeless future and the fear of prison and you had the motive that had driven him in a fit of depression to shoot himself.

Surely this combination of facts would convince the police to accept his death as suicide?

I paused to think about this carefully.

Dyer would be the perfect witness. He would tell the police about Vidal's financial position. He would express no surprise that Vidal had taken the easy way out. I wouldn't even come into the investigation. As a new member of the staff I wouldn't be expected to know anything about Vidal's affairs.

It seemed to me that this part of the plan must be foolproof.

I poured whisky into the glass and drank in two gulps. My heart was hammering and there was sweat on my face. Now the air conditioning was no longer functioning the room was beginning to get oppressively stuffy. The sound of the raging storm gave me a frightening sensation of being trapped in an normous drum on which some lunatic was beating.

The one man I feared was soundly asleep. Had Gesetti een prowling around the house instead of being in bed in a rugged sleep, I knew I wouldn't have had the courage to nove on to the next step of the plan.

Vidal was in his office, alone.

When Val had begged me to shoot her she had said, *No ne will hear the shot in the storm! You will be safe, darling. No one would suspect you.*

Yes! No one would suspect me!

I would go down silently to his office and walk in. The oom would be in semi-darkness. I would have the gun in my and by my side, out of his sight. I would say I wanted to talk o him about Val. He would irritably dismiss me. While I was rying to persuade him to listen to me I would move close to im, then jerking up the gun, I would shoot him through the ead.

I could do it! I had to do it! No one would suspect me! t would appear he had killed himself rather than go to rison.

Why wait?

Dyer was in bed. Gesetti was sleeping. There could be no etter moment. The screaming wind and the noise of falling rees would blot out the sound of the shot.

I thought of Val, sobbing and alone.

It would be over in a few minutes and she would be free. When the police investigation was over, we would be to-ether. She and I! After six years of waiting!

I got to my feet and started to the door, then stopped.

The gun!

I walked unsteadily to the desk, pulled open the drawer nd took out my brief case. Its flabby emptiness turned me old. Throwing the brief case aside with my heart hammer-ng. I peered into the drawer.

A tremendous clap of thunder shook the house.

The drawer was empty!

The gun was gone!

Nine

THE GUN had been in my brief case in the drawer. Now it had gone!

Who had taken it?

Vidal? Gesetti?

But neither of them knew I had the gun!

The shock of finding it gone, now that I was resolved to kill Vidal, was so great I felt as if I had been hit on the head. I dropped into my chair, resting my face in my shaking hands.

The sound of the storm was continuous. The screaming noise of the wind pounded on inside my skull.

Then who had taken the gun?

The only one who knew I had it was Val.

Val!

She had begged me to shoot her! Had she, in a mad moment, gone to my office while Dyer and I were checking the doors and windows, found and taken the gun?

I stumbled to my feet.

God! Had she killed herself?

In this infernal noise I wouldn't have heard the shot. I stood for a long moment in the grip of panic. It was at this moment when I thought I might have lost her for good that I fully realised how much I loved her, how much I depended on her to wipe out the memory of those six empty years when I had her only in my dreams.

I went out into the corridor.

Was she already dead?

Moving slowly, my heart hammering, I walked down to

er door. I put my head close to the door panel and tried to
sten but the noise of the raging hurricane blotted out every
ound.

Bracing myself, I opened the door.

Would I find her lying on her bed, lost to me forever?
Would she be bleeding from a dreadful wound in the head?

'Who is it?'

Her voice! She was alive!

I moved quickly into the room and closed the door. I
ood there, looking at her as she sat in a chair near the
urricane lamp, her hands in her lap, the lamp lighting the
se and fall of her lovely breasts and casting her tense white
ace into sculptured shadows.

'Oh, Val!'

I stumbled to her and fell on my knees, my head on her
highs, my hands around her waist.

Gently her fingers moved into my hair.

'Tell me.' Her voice was unsteady. 'Don't be frightened.
ell me I am free.'

I remained motionless. What had she said?

A tremendous clap of thunder shook the windows.

'Clay, darling . . .'

Tell me I am free.

I was still so shaken to find her alive, my brain refused to
unction.

'Clay!' Her voice sharpened. Her hands moved to my
houlders. She pushed me upright so we looked at each
ther.

'What has happened?'

Why was it her face seemed to me to be chiselled out of
marble? A trick of the flickering light?

'Give me the gun,' I said.

'Gun? What do you mean?'

I got unsteadily to my feet.

'Don't fool with me, Val! Give me the gun!'

'Gun? Clay! Pull yourself together! You told me you had
he gun!' Her voice turned shrill.

'It's gone! For God's sake, Val, don't torture me like this!
You took it, didn't you?'

'I?' She leaned forward, her fists clenched, her face the

153

colour of old parchment, her eyes wild and wide. 'No! Wha
are you saying? Isn't he dead?'

'No, I was going to kill him.' I turned away from her.
couldn't face her wild, despairing eyes. 'I had it all planned
It was to look like suicide. It seemed so simple. The motive
was there. They always look for a motive. He was being
threatened by prison or exile. He had lost all his money. Al
I had to do was walk in there and shoot him through the
head.' I moved further away from her. 'The gun has gone!

There was a long pause, then she said in a voice I could
scarcely hear, 'Who took it?'

'I was sure it was you.'

'No.'

I lifted my hands helplessly.

'What can I do now? I have no weapon. I can't fight with
him. He is far too strong.'

She drew in a long, slow breath.

'I told you,' She stared down at her clenched fists. 'There
is nothing to do. He is protected. Devils always are protected
Please go. If he found you here . . .'

'I promised to help you. I am going to help you!'

'Please go away!' She dropped her head in her hands and
began to sob.

'I will free you, Val!' I said frantically. 'By tomorrow you
will be rid of him!'

'Oh, go away! Spare me your empty promises. I told you
There is no solution. For God's sake, go away!'

I left her and returned to my office. I put the torch on the
desk and stood listening to the creaking boards guarding the
windows as the wind slammed against them.

Your empty promises.

That really hurt.

I went around my desk and sat down. The flickering lamp
cast ghostly shadows.

If Val hadn't taken the gun, who had?

I tried to remember when last I had seen it. Then I re
called opening my desk drawer and looking at the gun early
this morning. I hadn't looked at it since. So either Vidal
Dyer or Gesetti could have found and taken it.

I discounted Vidal immediately. I was sure, had he found

, he would have demanded an explanation: why had I a un in my desk? If Dyer had found it, I felt almost sure he ould have left it alone. I couldn't imagine Dyer touching ny gun.

Then it must be Gesetti!

I reached for the whisky, poured a stiff shot and drank it. he spirit bolstered my jumping nerves. Snatching up my orch, I went to the door and peered up the dark corridor nd then down the dark stairs. Moving swiftly, I descended he stairs and finally reached Gesetti's room. I paused to sten. He was still snoring.

For a long moment I hesitated, then turning the door andle, I moved into the room, leaving the door ajar.

There was a smell of stale sweat, sickly hair oil and cigar- tte smoke hanging in the darkness.

My heart was slamming against my ribs and my mouth as dry. If it hadn't been for the whisky I would have backed ut of the room.

Gesetti gave a sudden violent snort that lifted the hairs on he back of my neck, then he stopped snoring.

Had he come awake?

I remained motionless, sweat trickling down my face. I eard him heave himself over, grunt and then the snoring egan again.

Still I waited. Then satisfied he was truly asleep, I screened he bulb of my torch with my fingers and turned it on.

Keeping the shielded light away from the bed, I looked round the small room. Against the wall, close to me, was a hest of drawers. This would be the most likely place for him o have put the gun. Gently, I eased open the top drawer. It as full of fancy shirts, but no gun.

Closing the drawer, I pulled open the second drawer. As it ame open it gave a sharp squeaking sound that chilled my lood. I snapped off the torch.

The snoring stopped.

Inch by inch I began to close the drawer.

Then out of the darkness, Gesetti growled, 'Who the hell's here?'

I had the drawer shut now and I stepped quickly away rom the chest.

'It's all right.' I turned on my torch. My voice was a strangled whisper.

Gesetti was sitting up in bed. His snake's eyes glittered in the light of the torch. He looked as if he were about to spring at me.

'What do you want?' he snarled.

'I – I just looked in to see how you were.' I backed towards the door.

'Yeah?' His big fists rested on his knees. He was wearing his black open neck shirt. His heavy fat jowls were covered with stubble. 'I'll tell you. I've got a goddamn headache and I want to sleep. That's how I feel! Now piss off and don' come sneaking in here again or I'll kick the hell out of you!'

I stepped into the dark corridor and closed the door. I was so shaken I felt I was about to throw up.

As I started down the corridor, I saw a light coming from the stairs and the sounds of someone descending. I paused leaning against the wall.

Dyer came into view. He had on a dark blue dressing gown. The beam of his torch lit up the stairs.

I watched him. He went straight to Vidal's door, tapped opened it and paused in the doorway.

'Didn't I tell you I was not to be disturbed?' I heard Vidal bark.

'I'm sorry, sir, but Mrs Vidal . . . ' Dyer's voice trailed away.

'Well, What about Mrs Vidal?'

'She seems upset, sir. I heard her crying and sort of moaning. I thought you should know.'

'Very considerate of you, Dyer.' Vidal's voice was angrily sarcastic. 'You are getting as bad as Burden with this concern about Mrs Vidal.'

'I think you should see her, sir. She really sounds very bad,' Dyer said and moved back into the corridor.

'Goddamn it!' Vidal exploded. I heard him push his chair back violently and he came bouncing out into the corridor slamming his office door shut behind him. 'I'm getting good and tired of Mrs Vidal's damned hysterics!'

Pushing Dyer aside, he ran quickly up the stairs. Dyer hesitated, then followed him up.

I moved forward and paused at the foot of the stairs, seeing Dyer standing at the head of the stairs.

Then above the noise of the storm, I could just hear Vidal's angry shouting voice, but not what he was saying.

Then I heard a wild scream that made Dyer move forward.

I darted up the stairs as Dyer threw the beam of his torch down the corridor.

Val came bursting out of her room, her eyes wild, her hands groping forward.

I heard Vidal bellow, 'Come back here! Do you hear me? Come back here!'

She paused for only a brief moment to look back into the room, then she darted up the narrow stairs that led to the attics.

Vidal appeared in the doorway. His face was livid with ugly rage.

'Valerie! Come back!'

Then a great rush of wind came down the stairs, sending him staggering. I shoved Dyer aside and ran down the corridor. The violence of the wind caught me and threw me against the wall.

'The goddamn lunatic!' Vidal bawled. 'She's gone on the roof!'

He began to fight his way up the stairs. Clinging to the banister rail, hammered by the wind, I followed him to a broad landing.

Facing us was a doorway through which poured the wind and the rain. The door was slammed back against the wall.

'She's as good as dead!' Vidal bawled. 'No one could live out there!'

He struggled to the open doorway. Gripping the sides of the doorway, he peered out into the darkness while the wind and the rain lashed him. A vivid, blinding streak of lightning lit up the sky. The crash of thunder was deafening.

I tried to join him, but the wind slammed me to my knees. Vidal held on, his great strength defeating the pull of the wind.

Then I saw Dyer.

He came scrambling up the stairs on hands and knees, his

eyes bolting out of his head, his mouth half open. He passed me and then he drove forward in a flying tackle, his hand slamming against Vidal's broad back.

Caught off balance, Vidal pitched forward into the wind and the rain.

I had one brief horrible glimpse of him as the wind swept him from sight, then the torch I was holding slipped out of my fingers and began to roll down the stairs.

Darkness closed in as I heard Dyer, his breath sobbing through his clenched teeth, drag the door shut and slam home the bolt.

Val and Vidal were out there on the exposed roof, swept by the ferocious, deadly wind!

Had Dyer gone out of his mind?

He had bolted them out to certain death!

*   *   *

The sudden beam of Dyer's torch half blinded me. I could see he had set his back against the door. His face was as white as tallow and his lips kept twitching.

'Dyer! She's out there!' I shouted at him. 'Get away from the door! She'll be killed! I'm going after her!'

'Clay!'

The sound of her voice turned me to stone. Slowly, moved my eyes, my body rigid with shock.

Val was standing in the doorway of a small room to my right.

'It's all right, Clay.' A ghastly little smile hovered around her lips. 'It was the only way. You couldn't do it, so we did it.'

I stared from her to Dyer who was wiping his sweating face with his sleeve, then back to her.

'At last, I'm free, Clay,' Val went on, her voice trembling. 'He's gone forever.'

I couldn't grasp what she was saying. I felt so bad I thought I was going to pass out and I grabbed hold of the top of the banister rail to steady myself.

'You and Dyer? What are you saying?' My voice was a croak.

'You failed to help me, Clay, so Vernon has freed me.'

Bitter jealousy and anger swept over me. I faced Dyer.

'What is she to you to have done such a thing? You've urdered him!'

'Shut up!' His voice was a thin quaver. 'It's done!'

Then above the sound of the hurricane there came a olent hammering of fists on the door.

Dyer jumped away as if the door had turned red hot, his ce a mask of fear. He looked with horror at Val who emed to shrink, her face that of an old, terrified woman.

'Burden!'

Vidal's voice came through the door panels.

'He's alive!' I started forward but Dyer moved between me d the door.

'You want him dead, don't you?' he quavered. 'Leave m! He'll be swept away. You want Val to be free, don't u?'

I hesitated.

'Open the door, Burden!' Vidal's voice sounded fainter. urden!'

'He's calling to me,' I said stupidly.

'Let him!' Dyer's voice turned vicious. 'Go away! Leave is to me. He can't hold out much longer.'

'No!'

I saw my father, blood on his hands, as he skinned a rabbit. ll the old revulsion of violent death swept over me. I alised then that I would never have been able to shoot idal. And now, I knew I couldn't stand by and let him die t there. I had to save him! I just could not stand by, stening to him calling to me for help and do nothing.

The hammering on the door abruptly ceased.

'He's gone!' Dyer exclaimed.

Val hid her face in her hands.

I moved towards the door. Dyer grabbed hold of my arm. 'Get back!'

I shoved him aside and took hold of the bolt. I received a unning blow on the side of my head that made me stagger. s I spun around, Dyer hit me again, his fist thudding into y right eye, half blinding me.

Mad rage seized hold of me. All my pent up frustration

seemed to burst inside me. My fingers closed around Dyer
throat. He dropped the torch as he tried to drag my finger
away, but I was stronger than he.

He went down on his knees. I increased my grip. Vaguel
I heard Val screaming.

'Don't! Don't! Don't!'

Her screaming voice brought me to my senses. With
shudder, I threw Dyer from me, pushed Val aside, grabbe
hold of the bolt and wrestled it back.

The wind pounced as the door slammed open. I wen
down on hands and knees, peering into the wet darkness.

'Vidal!'

A vivid streak of lightning lit up the roof. I saw him. H
was lying flat, his fingers trying to get a grip on the wet roo
the wind moving him closer and closer to the sloping edge
Once there nothing could stop him from being swept away

I heard the door slam and the bolt go home. Dyer ha
locked me out! I didn't care. I had this compulsive urge t
save Vidal and I was going to save him! Lying flat, buffete
by the wind, I began to edge towards him.

'Vidal!' I yelled at him.

He looked around. The roof was lit by more lightning an
he saw me.

The wind suddenly flung me towards him. Grabbing hol
of a low wall that ran along the side of the roof, I manage
to anchor myself. I saw the wind shift Vidal towards th
sloping edge. I was within ten feet of him. I relaxed my gri
slightly so I was blown closer to him. Still holding on to th
wall, I stretched out my leg and his fingers closed around m
ankle.

The wind tore at us. I thought my grip must be broken
My arm felt as if it was being pulled out of my shoulde
socket. Vidal shifted his grip to my knee and heaved himsel
on top of me. As my grip was broken, he reached above m
and grabbed the wall. I began to slide away and I seized hol
of his jacket.

Half drowned, hammered by the wind, we lay panting
Then with incredible strength, Vidal began to claw his wa
back along the wall, dragging me with him. He kept movin
back until we reached the shelter of a chimney stack. Th

ind continued to roar around us but no longer dragged
t us.

Vidal leaned forward, his mouth close to my ear.

'There's another exit on the far side of the roof,' he
houted. 'If the door's locked, we're cooked.'

His face lit by a flash of lightning showed no fear. He
oked confident and calm which was a lot more than I felt.

'Stay here,' he went on. 'I'll try to get across.'

'You won't make it!' I shouted.

He didn't stop to argue. Keeping flat, he began to edge out
f the shelter of the stack. Instantly, the wind pounced on
im and if I hadn't caught hold of his arm, he would have
een swept away, across the roof and over the edge.

I dragged him back to shelter.

'So we stay here,' he said.

We stayed there, the warm rain beating down on us, the
ind howling around us, but at least we were in no immedi-
te danger.

The minutes dragged by: the most uncomfortable minutes
had ever lived through. There was no let up from the
iolence of the wind and the rain. We had to keep our heads
own to breathe. The almost continuous crash of thunder
eafened me. My mind was bludgeoned. I didn't even
onder how long we could remain as we were.

Then suddenly Vidal gripped my arm.

'Look!'

I followed his pointing finger. Across the far side of the
oof appeared the light of a powerful torch. The beam swept
he roof, passed near us, continued on, came back and found
s. For several seconds the beam held us, then abruptly went
ut.

'Gesetti!' Vidal shouted.

I felt a surge of hope.

Again the light appeared, then I saw Gesetti's squat figure,
t by the lightning, as he plunged towards us. The wind
hrew him flat and swept him across the roof. For a moment
thought he was going over the edge but another flash of
ghtning showed me he had a rope around his middle and
he rope was secured somewhere inside the doorway he had
ust left.

He fought his way nearer. Again the wind swept him back and again, but for the rope, he would have gone over.

'Hang on to me,' Vidal shouted.

As I caught hold of his jacket, he moved out of the shelter. We were swept towards Gesetti who grabbed hold of Vidal's wrist.

Then began the long and desperate struggle to get to the open doorway. Gesetti hauled on the rope, dragging himself, Vidal and myself inch by inch across the wet roof until we finally rolled through the doorway, out of the rain and the wind. As I leaned against the wall, my knees buckling, Vidal and Gesetti got the door shut.

'You took long enough,' Vidal said harshly. 'What the hell were you doing?'

Gesetti snorted.

'Getting the goddamn rope. If you think that was easy, have another think.'

'Where are they?'

'Trying to bust into your office.'

'That'll take them quite a time. Where do they think you are?'

Gesetti gave a snorting laugh.

'Dyer put on a big act and I fell for it. He got me out of bed, yelling you were out in the garden and in trouble so I go out in the wind and the sonofabitch locks me out. I saw you on the roof so I get the rope, kick in the back door and here I am.'

'They'll be busy for an hour or so. We'll take a shower and a change of clothes,' Vidal said. 'Here, Gesetti, find Burden something to wear. I'll be in Harris's room.' Taking a small flashlight from his pocket he went down the corridor and into a room at the far end.

Gesetti led me to another room. He lit a hurricane lamp then regarded me with his sneering snake's eyes.

'Go ahead, buster,' he said. 'Help yourself,' and he left me.

Unsteadily I went into the small bathroom, stripped off, took a shower and then returned to the room. Going to a closet I found a shirt and a pair of slacks that fitted me.

I moved like an automaton, my mind completely blank. I felt I was in the grip of a nightmare and what made this

162

nightmare so terrifying was the certain knowledge that when I woke from it, reality would be even more terrible.

The door jerked open and Vidal came in, wearing a dressing gown that trailed around his ankles.

'Come along, Burden, you need a drink.' He led me down the corridor and into the butler's sitting room.

Gesetti, wearing only a towel around his thick middle, was pouring whisky into glasses.

'Give Burden a drink,' Vidal said, sitting down, 'then get out.'

'Yes, boss.'

Gesetti gave me a tumbler half full of whisky and crushed ice, then left the room.

'Sit down, Burden,' Vidal said. 'Smoke if you want to. There are cigarettes in that box.'

I drank some of the whisky, then putting the glass on a nearby table, I sat down.

'You puzzle me,' Vidal said, staring at me. 'You saved my life.' He crossed one stumpy leg over the other. 'What made you do it? It interests me. Only an hour ago you were set to shoot me.'

I stiffened, staring at him.

'Tell me . . . why did you save my life, Burden?' he went on.

How could he have known that I was going to shoot him? Seeing my bewildered expression, he gave his short, barking laugh.

'There is nothing supernatural about me, Burden, in spite of what my wife has led you to believe and there is nothing I don't know about your association with her. When I discovered how dangerous she is, I had every room in this house bugged. I had your room and hers at the San Salvador hotel bugged. I have been listening for the past weeks to her plan to get rid of me with considerable interest, not to say admiration for her ingenuity.'

'What are you saying? Val? Dangerous?' I leaned forward to glare at him. 'It is you who are dangerous! Since you seem to know so much, you may as well know I have loved her for years and I still love her!'

'I know that. I'm sorry for you, Burden. Even now you

163

can't see that she has been using you as a cat's paw – as a sucker.'

Don't listen to him, I told myself. Val has warned you. This man is evil! He is trying to turn you against her.

'My poor Burden,' he went on after a long pause, 'you are in for a shock. Valerie is incapable of loving anyone. She just uses people for gain: as she used you, as she has used Dyer and as she tried unsuccessfully to use me.'

'I will believe nothing you say against her!' I shouted at him. 'She warned me! You are evil, vicious and ruthless! You have molested her under hypnotic influence! Nothing could be more despicable than that!'

'And yet you saved my life?' He lifted his eyebrows. 'Why did you do that, Burden?'

'Why did I? I have a conscience! I would rather be dead than to have your disgusting life on my conscience!'

'Very praiseworthy and yet you were tempted. She nearly convinced you, didn't she?'

'I won't discuss her with you!'

'Do you really believe that nonsense about me hypnotising her?' he asked. 'I admit, listening to the tapes, she is very persuasive but I assure you I have no talent for hypnotism.'

'I would rather believe her than you!'

There was no let up in the storm while we were talking. Thunder crashed and the wind howled and the rain hammered against the shuttered windows.

He got to his feet.

'Possibly they have broken into my office by now. Come along, Burden, see for yourself.'

He went to the door and opened it.

I sat there, hesitating. I recalled the scene of the landing when Dyer had shoved Vidal out on to the roof. I saw again Val's ghastly little smile and heard again what she had said: *It was the only way. You couldn't do it, so we did it.*

'Are you frightened of testing her, Burden? Scared she isn't the angel you think she is?' The sneer in his voice flicked me like a whip.

I got to my feet and followed him down the corridor to a door near the head of the stairs. He opened it and I found myself facing my office door.

'Wait a moment,' he said and went quickly into his room, leaving me alone in the dark with the sound of the hurricane crashing around the house.

He was away less than three minutes. His torch showed me he had pulled on a sweat shirt and slacks.

'Now, let us go down,' he said.

As we reached the foot of the stairs, I saw his office door stood ajar and a light showed. I was also aware that Gesetti was standing just outside the door. Seeing us, he came towards us.

'He's trying to open the safe, boss,' he said.

'That should prove difficult,' Vidal said. He was speaking in his normal voice. The sound of the hurricane turned it into a whisper. He caught hold of my arm and urged me to the half open door. 'Listen,' he said. 'Stay right where you are, but listen.'

I stood there, unable to see into the room, hearing nothing but the screeching wind and the rain.

Then above the storm I heard Val say, 'What the hell do you think you are doing? You said you could open it! Damn you! Open it!'

I scarcely recognised her voice which sounded harsh, strident and vicious.

'He's changed the combination!' Dyer shouted, his voice frantic. 'It won't open!'

'You'd better open it, you stupid bastard!' Val screamed. 'Do you think I've gone through all this for nothing?'

Every word she said made me cringe. I felt Vidal's hand on my arm.

'Let's go in, Burden,' he said. 'Let's surprise them.'

Before I could resist, he had shoved me through the doorway and he and I paused just inside the room.

Above the noise of the storm, I heard Val's scream.

Dyer was at the big wall safe. The light of three hurricane lamps played on him. Val was at his side, her eyes wide, her face like grey stone.

'No luck?' Vidal said as he moved into the room. 'Yes, I changed the combination. I thought it safe . . . r.' He gave his short barking laugh. 'Here's poor Burden. He still imagines you are an angel, Valerie.'

I was staring at Val. The bitter fury and fear in her eyes made her a stranger.

Then Gesetti came in.

The sight of him brought a faint scream from Val. Dyer who had been standing as if paralysed went limp and his face turned a greenish white.

Vidal walked over to his desk and sat down.

'Let us put Burden in the picture. As he saved my life, I feel that is the least we can do.' He waved to a chair near him. 'Sit down, Burden. Sit down you other two.'

There was a long pause, then Val sat down. Dyer looked fearfully at Gesetti and he too sat down, away from Val. I sat in the chair Vidal had indicated.

'Right,' Vidal said, looking directly at me. 'I will explain to you why these two nearly persuaded you to commit murder. In that safe that Dyer was trying to open are bearer bonds to the value of eight million dollars, the result of a deal I negotiated in Libya. The money, less my commission, belongs to the Government of El Salvador. Dyer assisted in the deal: he did the paper work. He knew the bonds were in the safe. I discovered several weeks ago that my wife was having an affair with him. I was not surprised. I have ceased to trust her for some time, but she is useful as a hostess and her infidelities – there have been others – don't worry me. However, it did worry me that my personal aide was being disloyal. I took the precaution to have the house bugged. It was a good move as I discovered they were planning to murder me. All their plotting is on tape. Dyer told Valerie about the bonds and assured her he could open the safe. For some time Valerie has been looking for an opportunity to get rid of me. As my widow she would have been reasonably wealthy, but when she learned she could pick up eight million dollars as well as getting rid of me the temptation was too great to resist. There is an interesting tape of her trying to persuade Dyer to kill me, but Dyer lacked the guts. He wanted her, he wanted the money, but he balked at murder. Valerie, on this tape, even discussed the possibilities of murdering me herself, but she flinched from a police investigation. Then you, poor Burden, arrived in Paradise City. When she insisted you should be her guide to El Salvador, I became curious but not

166

or long. There is another interesting tape which you can ear if you wish which records her and Dyer planning to make you their cat's paw. I don't recall her exact words but he intimated that you were gullible, that she would make love to you and revive your old passion for her, then over a short period she would lead you to believe that she was totally in my power and the only way she could get free was either to die herself or for me to die. Quite absurd, Burden. I did warn you. If you could believe that, you would believe anything. I arranged to have your room and hers bugged at the Intercontinental hotel. The tapes of her conversations with you were really astonishing, not to say diverting! Trilby and Svengali! My poor Burden, how stupid can you be? And all this talk about devils and me possessing her. Dyer, of course, was on hand to support her story. He even arranged that this old black quack should also support the story. Did you really imagine that old rogue was genuine? I have had him investigated. He would sell his mother for a quarter. Anyway, Valerie and Dyer succeeded in insinuating into your very gullible mind that the only way she could be free of my evil influence was for you to kill me. Having got that idea firmly fixed in your mind, they then gave you the perfect motive for an apparent suicide so you could feel safe after you had shot me.' He gave his short barking laugh. 'Her story that I had lost my money, that I am in trouble with the tax authorities and that I am about to flee to Lima is just hog's wash. However, you seemed so impressed with her story I took the precaution of removing your gun. Her talent for acting when she faked her trances which not only fooled you but the doctors, comes from being an actress in a third rate touring company some years before she became an efficient secretary. I am not asking you to believe any of this, Burden. You can hear the tapes. They will convince you.' He looked across at Val who was motionless, staring down at her hands. 'In spite of being on my guard, Burden, she very nearly outwitted me. I admit I underestimated her. I really did believe she had gone on the roof. I also underestimated Dyer. I didn't believe he had the guts to do what he did. Although they had no hope of laying their hands on the bonds, they did nearly succeed in murdering me.' He got to his feet. 'I think that will be enough for

167

tonight. Tomorrow, you can listen to the tapes. It will be of interest and will help pass the time while you sit out this hurricane. We will have to remain here for another two or three days: a tiresome necessity. I suggest you all keep to your rooms. Gesetti won't let you starve. None of you need be anxious. I will arrange a divorce. Dyer will look for other employment. As for you, Burden, I could find a place for you in my organisation, but we can discuss that possibility to-morrow.' He crossed to the door. 'Good night,' and followed by Gesetti, he left the room.

I looked at Val who was still staring down at her hands, then I looked at Dyer. His eyes shifted from mine and muttering something, he got up and walked stiffly out of the room.

I sat still. The noise of the hurricane still continued to hammer against the house.

'Val!'

She didn't look up.

'Tell me he was lying, Val, and I will believe you,' I said, my hands gripping the arms of my chair as I stared at her in sick despair.

Still she didn't move nor look at me.

'Val! Please! He must be lying! You couldn't do such a thing to me! I've loved you every minute of the six years we have been parted. I love you still! Tell me he is lying!'

Still she said nothing.

'For God's sake, Val!'

Suddenly she shook her head. In a low, hard voice, she said, 'He wasn't lying.'

Well she had said it. I drew in a long, shuddering breath.

'Val, darling, please listen to me. He is going to divorce you. At last you will be free of him. We can go away together. We can't get married because of Rhoda, but we can find work together. Darling, I don't care what you did. I don't care about Dyer. I love you! We can make a new life together.'

She looked up then, the bitter contempt in her eyes shrivelled me.

'A new life with you?' She started to her feet. 'With you, you weak, gutless jerk! I've never loved you! You have

ways been a stupid joke to me.' She was screaming at me
ow, her face contorted with spite and rage. 'Who wants
our gutless love? I hope to God I never see you again!'

She left me, my head in my hands with the nightmare that
ad now become a reality.

*   *   *

hunder shook the house while the wind screamed against
he boarded up windows.

I stared down at the rich carpet, hearing again those cruel
vords she had flung at me before leaving the room. *I have
ever loved you!* How it hurt to realise after so many years
hat I had been idolising a woman who only existed in my
esotted imagination! I sat there, hearing the hurricane,
eeling my life had come to an end.

'Hey, buster! Wake up!'

Gesetti's gravel voice made me lift my head. He was stand-
ng by me, his mouth twisted into a sneering grin.

I reared back.

'Get away from me!'

'Come on, buster, up on your feet. Beddy-byes now. I want
ou where I know where to find you. Move!'

The threat in his voice forced me to my feet. I couldn't
ear the thought of him touching me, but he did touch me.
His fingers closed around my arm: fingers like a steel claw
ind he led me from the room, out into the hall and up the
tairs and I went without resistance. When we reached the
upper landing, I saw Vidal standing in the doorway of his
room. He held a torch in his hand, the beam directed on the
loor. The reflection of the light showed me his set, hard
face.

I paused to stare at him.

A violent clap of thunder rocked the house as he stepped
back into his room and closed the door. There had been
something in his small, glittering eyes – something sinister –
that chilled me.

'Move, buster,' Gesetti said and nudged me on.

I had a sudden feeling of danger. I was now facing the
door into my room and Gesetti pushed the door open. A

169

presentiment that something terrible was about to happen brought me to a standstill. I spun around.

I felt a compulsive urge to rush down the stairs, fling open the front door and face the violent night – anything than stay a moment longer in this house.

Steel fingers gripped my arm and Gesetti's shoulder, as solid as a block of concrete, slammed against my chest. I went reeling back into the darkness of my room and the door slammed shut.

I groped around until I found the foot of the bed. The darkness was stifling. The noise of the hurricane hammered at me as I sank on the bed.

I began to shiver. Something was going to happen: something I was powerless to stop. I sat there, my fingers digging into the mattress, my heart slamming against my ribs while the hurricane banged and tore at the house.

Then I heard a faint scream. It was immediately blotted out by the roar of the hurricane, but I was sure it had been a scream.

I blundered to my feet and groped my way to the door. My sweating hand slid up and down the panel until I found the door handle. I turned the handle but the door remained immovable. I was locked in!

Again I heard the scream. This time there was no mistaking it. Val was screaming!

I threw myself against the door. I might just as well have thrown myself against a brick wall. I rattled the handle. I began to hammer on the panels.

The sound of my hammering fists was swept away by the noise of the hurricane.

Then the door shook as a tremendous blast of wind screamed down the corridor and I knew the door leading on to the roof had been opened.

'Val!'

I wrenched and tore at the door. It was immovable. Then the wind was cut off as the door leading to the roof was shut.

There was a long pause while I leaned against my door listening. All I could hear was the violence of the hurricane raging outside. I felt as if some living thing inside me had died. It was a feeling that left me weak and sick.

170

I groped my way across the darkness to the bed and sank
n to it. I knew instinctively that Val was dead. I knew
esetti had forced her on to the roof to be swept away by the
ind as Vidal could have been swept away but for me.

I could still hear her far away scream of terror echoing
side my head.

The door suddenly jerked open and Vidal, carrying a
urricane lamp, came in.

'An unfortunate accident, Burden,' he said, setting the
mp down on a nearby table. 'Valerie was deranged.' His
tle eyes, glittering with triumph, dwelt on me. 'You under-
and? The doctors know she was suffering from a nervous
eakdown. The hurricane unsettled her. She lost control of
rself and before I could stop her, she ran out on to the
of to be swept to her death.' His eyes never left my face.
ou understand?'

'You murdered her,' I said.

'Don't be stupid, Burden. It was an accident. And
yer . . . ' He gave his short barking laugh. 'He turned out
be a hero. Before Gesetti or I could restrain him he went
ter her only to be swept away in his turn. You understand?'

'You murdered both of them,' I said.

'No one attempts to take my life nor my money without
ying for it.' His voice was a sudden snarl. 'You won't be
volved, Burden. You were sleeping and heard nothing. I
ubt if the police will even question you. If they do, you
ow what to tell them. I'm giving you this chance because
u saved my life.'

Gesetti came to the door and stared menacingly at me.

The sight of him sent fear through me: fear that paralysed
e.

'It was an accident,' I said huskily.

'That's right,' Vidal nodded. 'People like those two don't
serve to live.'

He left me, and after staring at me for a long moment,
esetti turned and followed him.

I sat there staring at the flickering light of the lamp. Life
uld be empty without my dreams of Val. I had no one
w, then suddenly I thought of Rhoda. Even she, with her
ttishness, was better than nothing.

I sat there, listening to the violence of the hurricane, trying to assure myself that Rhoda was indeed better than nothing. The thought, stupid as it was, helped me to face the hours that stretched ahead.

THE END

HE DESTROYER: ACID ROCK by RICHARD
APIR and WARREN MURPHY

ickie Stoner was a fully-fledged groupie. She was nineteen,
d-headed, and worth one million dollars – *dead*! For Vickie
as the key prosecution witness in a politically important
al and someone, somewhere was willing to stake a fortune
prevent her testifying. CURE had orders to keep her alive
. not an easy mission – even for Remo Williams. And in
e screaming chaos of the world's biggest rock festival ever,
HE DESTROYER goes into action against the most
pert assassins of the underworld . . .

552 10017 X – 40p

HE DESTROYER: KILL OR CURE by RICHARD
APIR and WARREN MURPHY

man had been found with an ice-pick in his brain; the state
Florida was in an uproar; and CURE itself was in danger
being destroyed. A stupid and dangerous security leak
eant an unwelcome scandal in the highest government
ffices and threatened the very lives of everyone even
motely connected with CURE. Remo Williams had just
ne week to perform his own particular brand of miracle –
ne week before CURE and all its operatives would be
uietly and permanently erased . . .

552 10018 8 – 40p

YOU'VE GOT IT COMING by JAMES HADLEY CHASE

'The world is made up of smart guys who get rich and suckers who stay poor. I've been a sucker too long: now, I'm going to be smart. I know where I can put my hands on three million bucks, so I'm going to take them.'

Hi-jack a plane and grab 3 million dollars in diamonds . .
Harry Griffin liked the idea. Specially if it meant getting back at the airline that had sacked him.
Then there was Glorie. Harry was the ninth man in Glorie's life, and at her age she couldn't afford to lose him. So she fell in with the plan.
But Harry and Glorie were amateurs, they needed help the only trouble was, they picked the wrong man . . .

0 552 10138 9 – 60p

THE THINGS MEN DO by JAMES HADLEY CHASE

It was one of Harry's rules never to stop for hitch-hikers. But when he saw a pretty girl standing forlornly by her broken-down car, he decided to make an exception to his rule – an exception that was going to land him in a whole lot of trouble . . .
For the girl was Gloria Selby – rich and attractive, she had an uncanny talent for making money. And when she discovered Harry's business wasn't going too well, she presented him with a scheme to make him richer than he'd ever dreamed . . . and despite all the dangers, all the risk involved, Harry decided to take her up on her offer . . .

0 552 09934 1 – 45p

ARADISE ROAD by DAVID SCOTT MILTON

orter, Kitty and Eddie were celebrating Eddie's win in the
oxing ring when they saw them first. Yolande, the woman
as beautiful, with black hair and a pale face. Her husband,
att Nathan, was a tall, lean, and elegant, with soft sad
es and a gentle manner. Angel Amato, their companion,
as an ex-boxer – squat, with long dark hair and a punched-
. nose. Matt seemed friendly, eager to put Eddie under
ntract – and as one of the owners of the Paradise Hotel,
orter reckoned he had the means to do so. Porter, that
ening, had no way of knowing that this meeting with the
athans and Amato was to have a shattering effect on all
them . . .

552 10132 X – 75p

USSIAN ROULETTE by JAMES MITCHELL

hree highly efficient Russian exterminators were coming to
ondon. Their target? Callan. The reason? He'd been sold
t – by his own country . . . his own section. But more than
at, he'd been set up as a sitting duck for the K.G.B. He
uldn't get a gun . . . he couldn't get any money . . . and he
uldn't get a passport . . .

or the first time in his life Callan was the hunted not the
unter – the victim not the executioner. And he didn't like
– not one little bit he didn't like it – and if those bloody
ans thought he was going to make things easy for them,
ey had another think coming! He was going to fight – and
was going to fight the only way he knew how . . . dirty . . .
ry dirty . . .

552 09762 4 – 60p

A SELECTED LIST OF CRIME STORIES
FOR YOUR READING PLEASURE